WE THE PEOPLE

A PREMONITION

By Russell Razzaque

&

T. J. MacGregor

Cover illustrated by Megan MacGregor

TABLE OF CONTENTS

DEDICATION

For Tamara and Freddie

& For Megan and Rob

1

Even though this book is fiction, it's also a prediction. By the end of it, you'll realize the most important character is actually *you*. Then you'll be asked to make a choice, and this choice will determine the future of our species.

It is a choice we all must make.

"If I were to remain silent I'd be guilty of complicity."

Albert Einstein

PART ONE

Trajectories

"When injustice becomes law, resistance becomes duty."

Thomas Jefferson

ONE

February in Orlando reminded Luna Ochoa of her childhood in Caracas. The cool breeze combed through her long dark hair and carried the scent of the new planted gardens in the nearby park on Colonial Street. At this hour of the morning, pedestrians were out and about, hurrying to work. Many of them had their phones pressed to their ears or were scrolling through them. What had they done in the days before cell phones?

She turned into her building, a two-story structure where she'd worked for the last three years, since her thirty-seventh birthday. No sign outside, nothing to indicate what kind of business was inside. Her employer, Los Mejores - The Best - preferred it that way. Her office occupied the entire first floor and she shared it with her younger brother, Juan, who had taught her nearly everything she knew about computers and analysis of the information she and Juan gathered.

"*Hermana*," he called out as she breezed in. "You're early. You didn't stop for *cafecito?*"

"I forgot! Wow, that's a first."

Juan quickly stood, all six feet two of him, lithe and limber and so good-looking that a friend with whom she had worked in the FBI kept bugging her about an introduction. "Grab a seat, Luna. Take a look at this stuff I've been puzzling about. I'll get the *cafecitos*. You want anything to eat? An empanada?"

"I'm good. I had a bite for breakfast."

"Be back in fifteen."

She knew that meant he would be chatting away with the Cuban women who owned Havana Cafe. Mother and daughter. The mother, Margarita, had come over in the Mariel boatlift in 1982, when she was pregnant with her daughter, Elena. Luna sat at his desk, played the keyboard, and brought up the material he'd been studying.

For long, uncomfortable moments, she didn't know what she was looking at. She and Juan analyzed all kinds of data that the President and his minions had blocked. The list was extensive - weather, education, worldwide health crises, the rising number of homeless across the country, intelligence matters that the Department of Homeland Security had once been responsible for, citizenship issues, migration, the FAA, social security, Medicare and Medicaid, starvation worldwide, firing of federal employees who weren't white men……

She and Juan kept track of it all and had hacked into the administration's computer system to verify what these greedy bastards were doing. They regularly sent their findings to Leo Montoya, the CEO of Los Mejores, and he shared the information with his clients. Neither Luna nor her brother knew who his clients were, which was fine with them. She didn't want to know.

A few years ago, Leo had asked them to expand into AI, to find out what the government was doing with it or planning to do with it. She and Juan had both worked with it. At some point, though, AI had begun to freak her out so she'd backed off for a while. She wasn't sure what had disturbed her so deeply. Maybe it was just the idea that they were training a *machine* that might one day be able to run companies, countries, the world. But Juan kept pressing forward and she eventually had returned to it.

She typed in a command to return to what Juan had been seeing when she'd arrived. The screen abruptly went blank, then exploded with the image she'd seen when she had sat down. It looked like something from a movie, children shriveled up and dying from hunger and disease, adults dying from another pandemic as a man in the president's administration pronounced that the cure for an epidemic of measles was vitamin A and fish oil. She watched a war in the Middle East, watched a dictator grinning as a nuclear bomb exploded somewhere in Europe, watched the terrified and wounded and dying lurching, falling, their bodies melting.

Crowds of protesters in a city somewhere were shot down like target practice by masked soldiers with automatic weapons. Hundreds of bleeding bodies lay scattered in a plaza, a park.

ICE or some outfit like Hitler's SS dragged people from their homes, their cars, from schools. Incarcerated men and women screamed and wept as they were tortured by laughing guards.

Families were seized at the border, children taken from their parents, black men arrested and hung, young women taken somewhere to be impregnated.

In an underground bunker in another part of the world, billionaires cheered the horrific images on giant TV screens and toasted the president and other world dictators. She recognized two of these men, creators of apps that she used, along with millions of other people worldwide.

Now a massive tsunami crashed into the Florida Keys, wiping out everything from Key West to Key Largo, then Miami and Fort Lauderdale. On the Gulf coast, a tremendous hurricane that must have been five hundred miles wide with a tight, focused eye, tore apart the west coast of Florida and decimated the coasts of Alabama, Louisiana, Texas.

"Fuck." She typed STOP.

But the images didn't stop. More horror, more ruin, more cruelty. She ground her fist against her mouth, stifling a cry, as a group of billionaires drove jeeps and trucks into a forest somewhere and shot deer, bears, antelopes, tigers, even elephants. They laughed and laughed as they did it and then held up pieces of their trophies, grinning like the evil fucks they were.

Her hand fell away from her mouth and cries exploded from her. She couldn't hold back her horror and lurched to her feet and ran toward the door to find Juan, to escape. But he suddenly entered the office, holding two cups of Cuban coffee, a bag half-tucked in a pocket of his jacket and stammered, "My God, Luna, what…."

He threw open his arms to catch her, the cups of coffee hit the floor, and they stumbled back into the window. "I…I…The AI….scenes…." She couldn't find her voice. It had abandoned her.

Juan kept one arm around her shoulder and grabbed her hand, guiding her to the closest couch.

Luna sank into it and slapped her hands over her face, but she knew that Juan needed to see this, to see everything she'd seen and more. "Over...there." She bolted to her feet and ran back to the computer and stabbed her hand at the screen. "Watch..."

They both stood there, hands gripping the back of the chair, and stared. Images jumped around more rapidly now, yet each one was vivid, obvious. More hundreds of protesters being rounded up somewhere and gassed, shot, hung, set on fire. Across the planet, fires raged uncontrolled, unstoppable, planes plunged from the sky and crashed, astronauts in a craft or on the space station started choking, frantically seeking oxygen masks, instruments, the controls, dying.

The oligarchs and billionaires in their bunkers, their safe havens, had parties, celebrating their takeover of the planet while the rest of humanity suffered irreparably. At one point, sobs burst from Juan and he pressed the heels of his hands against his eyes. This time, she pulled him into her arms, hugging him tightly as she'd done when they were kids and he'd awakened from a nightmare. *Calmate, Juanito. Todo esta bien. Calm down, everything is fine.*

Except that nothing was fine. She knew it and so did Juan. He jerked away from her and threw out his arms at the computer, at the images that continued to march on by. His eyes were red, swollen, his dark hair so wild he looked like a guy coming out of a three-day drunken binge.

"That's our future, our fucking future," Juan whispered. "The AI is predicting our future."

New York fell, diminished to a ruin of concrete and wood and metal.

Buenos Aires burned.

The valley that held Caracas shook violently and everything collapsed - buildings, airports, streets, planes, car, homes, offices, markets, her old neighborhood. Las Mercedes. Luna's body crumbled. Her knees buckled and struck the floor. And everything went dark.

When she came to, on her side, she didn't know where she was, what had happened. She ached all over, her right side felt like it was on fire and she quickly rolled over, craning her neck to see if flames leaped off her body.

She wasn't on fire.

Luna rolled onto her back and lifted up on her elbows. Juan, crouched beside her, clasped her arm. "You scared me, *hermana*. You okay?"

Just a little sore...where I hit the floor."

"Thank God."

He scooped his phone off the floor. "I texted Leo. He wants a full report."

Now she remembered everything. She got up, still badly shaken by the images she'd seen, and returned to the computer. Stood in front it for a moment. The screen was dark, Juan had turned off the machine.

I turned off the AI for now," Juan said.

"What's Leo think about all this?"

"That AI predicted the near future. He and his team have been hoping for something like this. He says he would like to see a replay."

"Not me," she said.

Juan nodded. "Same here."

"I've never seen anything so...so horrifying, Juan. I'll write up the report. And include what I experienced."

"And I'll add my two cents to it." He pulled a chair out from the other computer and rolled it over to her. "Listen, given what we saw, maybe we should be, uh, making plans to move."

"The AI didn't give a time frame, did it?" a"Not that I saw. Leo asked the same thing."

"For the time being, I think we should stay here in Orlando. It's 112 feet above sea level," Luna said.

"I wasn't thinking of hurricanes or tsunamis." Juan leaned forward, elbows propped on his knees. "But quakes. Like Cara…" He choked up, unable to finish the word Caracas. When he continued, his voice fell to a whisper. "Shit, that was heartbreaking. Or the raging fire that destroyed B.A.…."

Their father had been Argentinian, from Buenos Aires.

"And the protesters shot and jailed and set on fire…people pulled for their homes and cars…" His voice broke again and she grabbed his hand and held tightly.

"I'm here, Juan. Text Leo. It's faster," she said.

"Good idea." He scooted his chair back to the other computer and went to work.

They were on a private server that was heavily encrypted, so they didn't hesitate emailing and texting him. Since texting was more immediate, she used the computer to do that. Faster.

Hey Leo. This whole AI thing happened suddenly and unexpectedly and was a total shock. The images were vivid, in full technicolor, violent, detailed, horrifying. No specific time frame but my sense was that it's soon. Juan says you want to see a replay. We'll pass on that.

Too traumatic, heartbreaking.

It wasn't just the climate change events, but the unconscionable acts of violence against fellow humans.

At some point, I just broke down, sobbing hysterically. I lost consciousness. Haven't ever seen anything like this. Juan sending notes too.

"Sent my text," she said.

"Just finishing mine."

Luna pushed back from the computer and went over to the small fridge against the wall for a bottle of water. Through the window that faced the street, the shadows looked longer, the light was late afternoon. Weird, she thought. How had so much time passed so quickly? Before the AI had exploded with revelations, Juan had returned with coffee from the Havana Cafe. Yet the light outside told her it was late afternoon, closing in on dusk.

She helped herself to a container of water and gulped at it as she walked back to the computer. Leo had responded already. She quickly sat down, set the water to the side, and added her brother's name to the message.

14

Luna, thank you for the info. Got Juan's text, too. Dios mio, am eager to see the replay. But more than that, am eager to see the 2 of u. Will be in Orlando tomorrow around 10 AM. Let's all meet at Havana Cafe. Table by window.

She thought a moment, then typed: *What do you intend to do with this info, Leo?*

Try to get a time frame, then issue a warning.

Through who or what? They shut down NOAA, most weather and news outlets.

We created our own.

News to her. She glanced over at Juan. "Did you know about that?"

"Nope."

Weather and news apps?

Yeah. Weather app called Peekaboo. We hired NOAA employees who had been fired. The news app is nearly done. We'll be transparent about the warnings, that the predictions were made by AI.

Does AI have a name?

Not yet. Got any suggestions?

The People. It's people who trained AI

and...then...At first, Leo...I thought it was conscious. But...it's not. It's all logic and...somehow, that's even more frightening.

Juan broke in. *AI was trained by men and women and that combination gave us the predictions of the near future.*

Precognitive? Leo asked. *Is that what you're saying, Juan?*

I don't know. Maybe in a way we don't understand yet.

All right then, meet you 2 tomorrow morn, 10, Havana Cafe.

We'll be there.

* * * * *

When they finally left the building, the darkness that covered Colonial Street was broken up by lights from buildings and businesses, street lamps, headlights. They had their computers in their packs and the office was locked up tight against intrusion. The security cameras were on, inside and out. Just in case. Yeah, just in case their server wasn't as secure as they believed.

"I'm starving," she remarked.

"I need a drink."

"Same. Mickey's has good food and inexpensive wine."

"Then that's our go to place."

Two blocks later, they entered Mickey's, where a band was warming up, most of the tables were taken, and they managed to find a couple of seats at the end of the long, curving bars. Raul, the Latino bartender from Bogota, came right over. "*Ochoas, bienvenidos. Como andan?*"

"*Con los dos pies, amigo,*" Juan replied.

The greeting always made her smile. Raul literally asked, *How're you walking?* And Juan replied, *With both feet.*

Even Raul laughed, then leaned forward, his bushy dark brows sliding together so they formed a thick bridge above his chocolate colored eyes. "What the hell is going on?" "You a citizen, Raul?" she asked.

"Green card. Is ICE rounding us up yet?"

"Not yesterday or today," Juan replied. "But maybe next week. *Con cuidado, amigo.* If you hear they're around, stay inside. They don't have warrants. They can't break into wherever you are. I think many

17

of them are part of the president's private army."

"*Cabron*," Raul spat.

Then Juan ordered a Merlot for her and a straight rum for himself, and she ordered fish sandwiches and gazpacho soup.

Juan, who seemed to know every Latino in town, went over to a table where a couple sat and joined them. She felt a brief stab of loneliness that she didn't have anyone in her life except her brother to whom she could turn now for comfort. No husband, no lover, no one with whom she could share her deepest fears and uncertainties.

When she'd worked at the FBI, she'd been dating another agent but that had ended when the president's goons had eliminated her job along with 2,000 others. Ultimately, it had worked out to her advantage. Leo Montoya had hired her two days later and a week afterward, had hired Juan, who had gotten fired from his job in the IT department at the University of Florida, a purge by the Florida governor. He was another of the president's minions, just as despicable as he was.

These men were using the tried-and -true playbook of all autocrats. From Hitler and Mussolini, Pinochet to Chavez and Maduro, Hussein to Castro and Gaddafi and Franco, the playbook was about seizing control. They usually started with the press and the military, then education, books, health and human services, and individual rights like free speech and due process. They squeezed and squeezed, doing everything they could to suffocate joy and happiness and the ability to think for yourself.

She pressed her knuckles against her eyes and ordered another Merlot.

TWO

Jake Kessler knew he was stuck in a dark, terrible place in his life but didn't't know what to do about it. The time for rectifying things was long gone. So here he was, 44 years old, renting a two-bedroom apartment on the outskirts of Orlando, editing copy for a glossy magazine, the kind his ex-wife bought regularly and devoured.

The article was about trending places in the central Florida area - which, according to the magazine, extended as far east as Daytona Beach, one of the spring break playgrounds. Never mind that Disney World accounted for the bulk of tourism here. Hell, if it weren't for Disney, this area would just be some Podunk town way north of Miami.

He sent off the article to his editor in New York and put his computer to sleep. It was 7:25 p.m. He hadn't eaten dinner. He hated cooking for himself. When he was married, he'd done most of the cooking with whatever his wife had bought. She'd loved steak and pork, which he hadn't eaten in at least twenty years, so she usually had bought fish and lots of veggies and fruit for him.

He rubbed his eyes and folded his arms on his desk and rested his head against them. Five minutes, he thought. His eyes ached. He couldn't sleep through an entire night, hadn't been able to since he'd gotten fired from *Florida News* two years ago. The state's most prestigious newspaper had been bought by one of the governor's billionaires buddies and turned into a right-wing rag. He'd been fired the next day because his obsession and expertise were in highlighting corruption in the current political environment, state and federal, and he'd focused on the 800 billionaires who now ran both.

It didn't matter that he'd won a Pulitzer.

He'd loved his job at *Florida News,* and when he was *targeted* by this corrupt federal administration and he and his family had received death threats, his wife had divorced him and taken their teenage daughters with her. Then he'd gotten fired and had to sell the home where he and his family had lived for years. He and his ex had split the money and he'd moved to this nondescript apartment outside of Orlando. She now rented a house in the area.

He'd gotten the job at the glossy magazine because the editor was a long-time friend but even she had hired him with a condition: *no politics, Jake. Can't afford to lose my job.* More than his need for the work, he'd craved a distraction, so he'd taken the job.

So much for freedom of the press.

His stomach rumbled with hunger and he lifted his head from his arms and glanced at the clock on the wall. Nearly eight. Time to eat. And he could definitely use a drink. He got up from his desk, grabbed his cell phone and wallet, shrugged on a jacket and left the building.

Outside, the cool weather felt invigorating and woke him up. The night was utterly clear and out here, away from the city, the stars and rising moon owned the sky. He got into his SUV and headed downtown.

He remembered that not long after he and Kate were married, they had sat in their backyard on nights like this, sprawled in beach chairs that folded back so they could take in the sky. Something about that sprawling grandeur had encouraged them to think differently about what they both hoped for the marriage. A family, certainly, but also doing work about which they were passionate that also would benefit the larger world somehow, in some way. Kate had been a social worker until she'd gotten pregnant and then she'd turned to wedding planning, which she could do at home. She enjoyed it, was good at it, and as their daughters had gotten older, she'd rented an office downtown. And that was the where the goons from the federal administration initially had threatened her.

First, it was the calls.

Then the emails.

Then, one afternoon while Jake was working in the back room of her office, one of these goons dropped by. Jake spotted him first on the security cam, a short, squat guy in his thirties in jeans and a tee-shirt, a kind of little man in black, not the least bit intimidating until he opened his mouth.

" Kate Kessler?"

" Yes, how can I help you sir?"

He placed his hands at the edge of her desk and leaned forward and at that point,

Jake hurried into the front room. "Get the fuck away from her."

The man apparently had thought Kate was alone in the office and wrenched up and patted the air with his hands as he moved back toward the door. "Jake Kessler. Back off from your lies and fraud or your family is going to disappear."

Before he reached the door, Jake lurched toward him, grabbed the front of the man's shirt and threw him against the wall. Kate screamed for him to stop, please, so Jake hurled open the door and pushed the shit into the street.

Jake shook the memory away. The president's and governor's minions now left him alone. And Kate said she and their daughters felt safe living in Deland.

But the very thing that had happened to him and his family was happening to others whom the president or the illustrious Florida governor perceived as personal enemies. Attorneys, physicians, veterans, other journalists, politicians, filmmakers, fired state and federal employees who had sued one or both of them. The list was long. And he suspected that the cost to many of them would be what it had been for him - the loss of everything meaningful.

When he reached the door of Mickey's, he felt depressed, almost hopeless. But the live music inside the place cheered him somewhat and he was delighted to see such a large crowd. It meant these people were trying to live ordinary lives in spite of the horror around them. He spotted an empty seat at one end of the bar and made a beeline toward it.

As he sat down, a server hurried over. "Food or drinks for you, sir?"

"Both."

"Perfect. Here's a menu, just signal me when you're ready."

"I already know. The fresh fish sandwich, a side of fruit, and the tallest glass you have for bourbon."

"Got it," the man said.

He started to turn away, but the woman next to Jake spoke up. "Raul, *otro vino, por favor.*"

"You bet, chica."

Jake glanced at her, a Latina brunette whose pretty face looked ravaged with fear, anxiety, disgust. "Bad day?" he asked.

"You've got no idea." She turned her head toward him, those dark chocolate eyes suddenly crinkling at the corners. "Tallest glass for bourbon? Bad day?"

"You've got no idea."

She didn't quite laugh, but his response elicited a quick smile from her. "Given all this shit that's going on, it's tough to be optimistic."

A TV on the wall was tuned to the news and as she spoke those words, they both stared at it, at the images of hundreds of protesters in Manhattan being gassed, beaten, dragged away. The woman slammed her fist down over the TV's remote control that the server had left on the counter. "Can't. I just can't stand seeing it."

"Agreed. I'm Jake Kessler."

"Luna Ochoa."

"*Un placer*," he said in his awkward Spanish.

"*Lo mismo*. And yes, I'm a citizen, so ICE isn't a threat. Not yet, anyway." She paused, frowning. "Wait a minute. *Jake Kessler*? The same Kessler who used to write for *Florida News?*"

"Yeah, but don't tell anyone or you may find yourself threatened. Or rounded up."

"What happened? Were you fired for the political stuff you wrote?"

"Sure."

"I loved your pieces, Jake. Read them daily. And it turned out that you were absolutely right."

She gulped at the wine the server had set in front of her and signaled him for another. She clearly wasn't a drinker and was gulping at the wine to obliterate her bad day. "What do you do?" he asked.

"Work with computers. My brother and I." She

motioned at a man sitting with several other people near the window, all of them huddled forward toward the middle of the table so they could hear each other over the music. "Curious about something, Jake. What do you think of AI?"

"Didn't think much about it all until after I got fired. Now I write for a women's beauty magazine and use it frequently." He shrugged. "I'm just not much of a women's beauty writer."

The man she'd pointed out as her brother now came over to the bar, slung an arm around Luna's shoulders and said something so rapidly in Spanish that the only part of it Jake caught was *Me voy a ....* *I'm going to.*

"Jake Kessler, my brother Juan."

"Pleasure, amigo," Juan said, and shook Jake's hand.

Then he left with the group of people he'd been sitting with and Luna stared after him briefly, then turned back around and reached for her fresh glass of wine. "Do you think AI can predict the future, Jake?"

Of all the questions he'd thought she might ask, this one didn't even appear on his list. But he sensed her concern about it. "No idea. I've just used it to round out my articles so it sounds like I know what

I'm talking about when it comes to women's beauty."

She sipped at her wine.

" Why? Do you think it can?" he asked.

" I...I... *know* it can." She tossed a $20 bill on the counter, grabbed her bag, her jacket, and fled the bar.

It happened so quickly that when Jake got up to go after her, he realized he hadn't paid his bill. Hadn't even gotten his bill. He signaled Raul, who came over and glanced briefly at the door, then said, "Thirty bucks should do it. Listen, she and Juan are friends of mine. Can you, uh, make sure she doesn't drive? She's had a lot of wine. I'll alert Juan."

Jake set three $10 bills on the counter, scooped up his things and hurried out of the bar, hoping that Luna hadn't gotten too far. He spotted her stumbling up the road and walked quickly after her. He caught up to her, took her hand. "Hey, it's okay. We're on the same side of this political stuff. Can I give you a ride home?"

" I work just...just a couple blocks up the road."

" And I'm parked two cars from right here."

" You don't mind?"

" No, of course not."

"Thanks." She gripped his hand more tightly. "I had way too much wine. Do I sound drunk, Jake?"

Nah, but you were stumbling."

She rubbed her free hand across her forehead, her eyes. "When I feel like this, I should…eat a gummie. Smoke some weed. I shouldn't drink. But the gov overturned the medical weed thing in this state. And he instructed his kiss ass legislature to prevent *us* - the *voters*, the *people* - from voting on amendments like making weed legal. But it's just fine to have an open carry law. And oh, if there's a shooting at your school, you have our prayers and deepest condolences."

Some laws had changed in the aftermath of the 2018 shooting at Marjorie Stoneman Douglas High School in Parkland, Florida. The state legislature had raised the minimum age for purchase from 18 to 21 and eliminated the loophole that allowed private gun sales without background checks. Those were the two biggies in his mind. They also banned bump stocks, expanded the amount of required information on background checks and imposed a three-day waiting period for handguns.

But when the governor came into office, he overturned all those laws and implemented two of his own: the legal age for purchasing a firearm was changed to eighteen once again and open carry became legal.

He pulled into a parking spot in front of her building and they both got out. "Need help?" he asked.

"I look that bad, huh? Shit." She played the keypad to her right and the door swung open. "C'mon in. Welcome to Los Mejores. That's the company name." She swung her arm through the door.

"Security cams in there?" he asked.

Sure. Juan and I...dismantled all of them. Leo called us on it..."

"Your boss?"

"Yeah. Owner of the business. I told him I wouldn't work in a place where I was spied on. The cams in here are permanently dead."

Only then did he enter the office.

She drew the blinds across the front windows, flicked on an overhead. Compared to his home office, this place struck him as large. No, immense. And comfortably furnished with couches and tables placed strategically among four desks, a small kitchen with a fridge and stove and cupboards, a dining area tucked off against a wall, a pair of wall TV screens. He counted four desktop computers and printers, a closet, bathroom with a shower, and suspected that Luna and her brother often stayed here overnight. Maybe they actually lived here.

" You and Juan live here?"

" It'd sure be cheaper than paying mortgages on two places. But Leo wants personal and business separate. We just stay here sometimes."

She moved around quickly, gathering up her things, then went over to the fridge and brought out two aluminum bottles of water. She passed him one. They each twisted the caps, drank, and she said, "Do you want to see the AI predictions?"

" There's a list?"

"Uh, no. There are images."

" I'd love to see them. Thanks, Luna."

" Hey, it's the least I can do to repay you for giving me a ride here and then home." She headed for the front door and motioned for him to follow. Outside, she said, "You can watch it at my place, where I know there aren't any security cams."

* * * * *

She lived in what felt like the middle of nowhere.

31

He turned onto an unpaved dirt road that led into a thicket of trees somewhere off north I-4. The road had a name -Junger Forest- and on the way along it, they passed just half a dozen houses, all of them set on large lots - three to five acres, he guessed.

Her place was the fourth one in, an A-frame with towering ceiba trees in the front yard and walls of glass at the front, windows closed off by curtains. "Just pull up in front."

" Pretty remote," he remarked.

" Just the way I want it. After the president's minions fired nearly everyone in the FBI, I sold my place in town and bought out here."

" What did you do there?"

" I was an agent. For more than a decade."

She opened the door with just a key and they went inside. She flicked on lights as they entered the living room at the back of the house, where the sliding glass doors faced a lake illuminated by moonlight. "Gorgeous," he remarked.

She set her stuff on the living room coffee table and went into the connected kitchen. "Ice tea? Lemonade? Cold water?"

" Anything, thanks."

Jake sat at the table and when she emerged from the kitchen, she set a glass of lemonade in front of him, then opened her computer and set it up. "This is a replay of what we saw. But I...I can't watch this again. It's...devastating."

She played the keyboard. When images started appearing on the wall to his right, Luna headed toward the porch with her tall iced tea, walked out and shut the sliding glass doors behind her. Jake sank onto the couch and watched the utter horror of the future unfold in front of him.

* * * * *

Luna sat on her balcony for what felt like hours.

She wished she had a pet - a dog, a cat- some cuddly creature she could slip her arm around. Growing up in Caracas, she and Juan always had dog and cats who were members of the family. But when she'd entered the adult world of eight or ten-hour work days, she hadn't owned a pet and that had seemed like a good thing. Now, as she violated Leo's primary rule to maintain an NDA about all data Los Mejores retrieved, she felt bad that Jake was watching those images alone. She didn't hear screams or shrieks yet, no hollers, no sudden appearance here on the balcony.

At some point, though, he did appear, opening

those porch doors. He looked shaken as he walked out to where she sat, pulled over the only other chair out here, and sank into it. He worked off his shoes, unzipped his jacket, and for the longest time said nothing. Once, he brought out his phone and looked at the temperature.

"I feel like I'm burning up from the inside out," he remarked. "But my vastly diminished weather app says the temp is somewhere between 50 and 55."

"See if you can get into an app called Peekaboo."

"What is it?"

"Supposedly a weather app, but I'm honestly not sure. Boss Leo and his team created it."

While Jake tapped away at his phone, she brought out her iPad, downloaded the Peekaboo app, and poked around on it. Damn good, she thought, and then a hidden link appeared on her screen for an app called *The News They Try to Hide.* The image showed a line of Venezuelan immigrants, all in white shorts and white shirts, arms bound behind them, legs shackled, their heads held down by the individual ICE agent escorting them out.

The fact that they were Venezuelans who probably had voted for this president and this governor sickened her.

"Jesus, did you see this news app?" Jake exclaimed. "And the image?"

" Just...found it."

" I'd like to go to work for you," he said. "I think I can contribute to what you're doing."

Yes, he undoubtedly could. "Leo will be at the office at ten tomorrow morning. That would be an ideal time for you two to meet. I know he's familiar with your writing."

" Do you have a way to get back into town tomorrow?"

" Yeah. Juan's old VW Bug is in the garage. His townhouse only has a one-car garage, so he keeps it here rather than paying for parking. I can get into work. Just don't let Leo know that you've seen the images I violated our NDA by letting you see it."

" No problem. Should I update my resume?"

She laughed at that. "Uh, not necessary. Like I said, he's familiar with your work."

He stood, rapped his knuckles against the table. "It's late, I better shove off. I'll get there tomorrow before ten."

She glanced at the time on her iPad. "It's past

midnight, Jake You're welcome to stay in the guest room."

"Wow, thank you. My place is about twenty miles from here. I've got a pack in my car that always has clean clothes, toiletries and stuff."

"Perfect. To be honest, after today, I'm a bit freaked out to stay here alone. I appreciate the company, Jake."

"You need a guard dog out here, Luna."

They both left the porch and went inside. She locked the porch door, drew the blinds, and showed him the guest bedroom and adjoining bathroom. By the time she fell into bed, exhaustion had eaten into her bones.

She woke suddenly at 5:30 to a buzzing on her watch. One glance at it and she scooped her cell off the mattress beside her. "Leo." She cleared her throat. "It's kinda early."

"Yeah, I know, I'm sorry. Something's come up. I'm maybe 15 minutes from your place. Okay if I stop by?"

She quickly sat up. "Sure. Of course. But Jake Kessler is staying in the guest room and..."

"*The* Jake Kessler?"

" Yeah. And he'd like to work for us, Leo."

" My God, yes, tell him yes. Be there in twelve minutes."

They disconnected and Luna turned on the bedside lamp, scrambled out of bed, did her bathroom routine and dressed. She hurried up the hall to the guest room, but the door was open and she found Jake sitting in the kitchen, going through his notes.

" Hey, Leo's going to be here shortly. Not sure what's going on. I told him about you, that you wanted to work with us, and he said yes, yes, sign you up."

Jake bolted to his feet. "Fantastic. Need to change clothes."

"I'll start the coffee."

She glanced at her watch. TICK-TOCK. Whenever Leo gave her a time, he arrived promptly. She had less than five minutes.

She started the coffee, turned on her iPad and computer, hurried to the front door. She unlocked it and stood on the porch in the brisk night air, her jacket zipped up. She felt certain this surprise visit was connected to Leo having watched the images of the AI's predictions.

Sure enough, exactly at 5:42, a dark SUV pulled into her driveway and Leo quickly got out, alone. He always traveled alone. He was a lean six feet, dark hair, a Latino in his late forties who spoke several other languages as well as he spoke English and Spanish. He'd made a ton of money in real estate and that wealth funded Los Mejores - computers, his primary team, the information networks, employees like her and Juan, and the fired federal employees he'd hired. She didn't know much about his early life or how he'd started Los Mejores. At one time he'd been married, now had a son at Yale, but his focus was this work.

He trotted up the driveway and she hurried down the steps to meet him. He hugged her hello. "That images...Luna..." He stepped back. "I..."

"Let's get inside."

THREE

Jake sensed his life was about to slam into a vast and sweeping change. After all, when Leo Montoya walked through the front door of Luna's house, it was barely six in the morning, in a house in the middle of virtually nowhere that was owned by a woman Jake had met just hours ago in a bar. It felt like synchronicity was at play here.

Luna introduced them and the two men didn't shake hands. Instead, Leo slung an arm around Jake's shoulders. "Amigo, you're hired and I want you to know how honored we are to have you on our team. I was one of your huge fans." He paused. "What can you do for us?"

"That depends. What're you doing? I brought up Peekaboo and The News They Try to Hide. What else do you have?" Luna came up behind them. "Guys, the table. Where the computers are."

Once they were settled at the table, Leo turned to Luna. "Did you show him the images?"

"Bet your ass. Violated the NDA with good reason."

"Good." Leo looked at Jake. "And what did you think?"

"That we're fucked unless we do something. What do *you* have in mind?"

"We work against all this from the inside out," Leo replied.

Luna brought cups of coffee over to the table with containers of sugar, milk, and a platter of breakfast goodies. "Please explain how we do that," Luna said.

"I'm going to show these images to the rest of my team, get their take on it, and then decide which direction we should take." He paused. "But right now, we're going underground - literally. I've procured an underground area that should be safe for several thousand people, maybe more."

"Where?" Jake asked. "In Colorado? Inside Mount Shasta? Somewhere in Washington state?"

"I'll alert you two and Juan to that very soon. But right now, it looks like Kevin Philips is onto us and that worries me."

Philips. Jake had met him before he'd been promoted to the head of the Artificial Intelligence Threat Management - AITM - in the presidential administration. Back then, Philips worked as some lower IT person whose unwavering loyalty to the president had guaranteed a promotion of some kind. He was one of the last interviews Jake had done for *Florida News.* "How do you know?" Jake asked.

"His latest post on *Dawn.*"

The president's social media site. Jake stayed away from it most of the time because the comments to whatever this idiot posted were disgustingly positive and supportive. The president's base was like that of Jim Jones, the infamous cult leader of The People's Temple in Guayana, who had convinced his followers to down a fruit drink that had been laced with cyanide. The mass suicide was supposed to keep them safe from a raid.

"Here, take a look." Leo handed Jake his phone.

The post had gone up last night, just after midnight:

It's come to my attention that a computer company in Orlando has access to a wealth of AI data that private companies are not permitted to have. And just in case you doubt that, please see the president's latest executive order about this. I have ordered the company to turn over their data in 72 hours or face criminal charges.

"You're aren't specifically named," Jake said, handing the phone to Luna.

"I received an email." Leo brought out two folded sheets, passed one to Jake, the other to Luna.

The Office of Artificial Intelligence Threat Management

Director: Kevin Philips   Mr. Montoya,

It has come to our attention that your company. Los Mejores, has access to a large database of AI intelligence and is in clear violation of the President's most recent executive order. You have 72 hours to turn over this material to my office or you will be criminally charged.

Sincerely,

Kevin Philips

Luna passed the printed email back to him. "Maybe we should vacate the office in Orlando, Leo."

"I've already given notice and found a new office in Sanford. An apartment, actually. In a large neighborhood. A couple of men on my team are headed there this afternoon to move everything that's ours. Here's the address for the new place." He handed them each a card with the address jotted on it. "Be sure to tell Juan, Luna. I don't want to use texts or emails until our system is checked thoroughly. We haven't yet discovered how this asshole Philips knew anything about our AI database."

"Maybe it's just based on supposition," Jake said. "It's this president's MO. Threaten and bully and then back off."

Leo nodded. "Yeah, I know. But I'm not willing to take the risk. You'll be paid in cash, Jake. And Luna, the same goes for you and Juan from here on in. I don't want my employees paying taxes into this corrupt system. Or paying for social security now that the president and his billionaire minions are dipping into the SS funds."

"That could be a problem with our banks," Luna remarked.

Jake nodded. "It could be, yes, if you deposit more than ten grand at a time."

"Jake's right. If it becomes an issue for you or Juan, Luna, just let me know."

He pushed to his feet. "You should probably swing by the office downtown first when you leave here, make sure all your personal belongings are gone. I can meet all of you at the new place in Sanford at three this afternoon."

"I'll be there," Jake said.

"Ditto," said Luna.

They walked to the front door with Leo. "And this afternoon, we'll talk about all this at greater length."

Then he was gone and Jake glanced at his watch. "I'd better go gather up my stuff and get going. See you at your old office around ten?"

"Perfect."

"I like Leo."

"He's terrific to work for. I'm happy he hired you, Jake. We need additional help. So I guess we don't text, given what he said. Hope it's safe for me to call Juan and tell him to meet me at the Cuban cafe. That doesn't reveal much."Unless the president's minions had tapped her and her brother's phone.

* * * * *

Thanks to morning rush hour traffic, the drive back to his place took longer than usual. Jake pulled up in front of his apartment building shortly before eight a.m. and was surprised to see Max Oakland get out of the car parked at the curb in front of him.

"Max, this is a surprise."

"We need to talk, man."

"Sounds urgent."

"Yeah. It is."

"Let's go inside."

During the years that Jake had worked for *Florida News,* Max had been one of his primary informants at the FBI. He had worked as a fed for twenty years and hadn't been fired yet by the president, probably because he tended to be so engaging. As the guy in charge at the bureau's Central Florida office, he kept a low profile. He was in his early fifties, nearly bald, and had a quick, uneven smile.

Inside the apartment, Jake dropped his stuff in a chair. "Have a seat, Max. What's up?"

Max pulled out a chair at the kitchen table, ran his hand over his head. "Okay, this is…fuck it. I'll get right to the point. Kevin Philips assigned one of the agents under me to keep tabs on Luna Ochoa and you were seen entering her office with her last night, then the two of you left together. I was her boss when she worked at the bureau, Jake. She was a whiz at IT stuff, a highly respected analyst. But the president's minions decided that she and seven hundred other agents were immaterial to the functioning of the bureau so they were fired in the first wave. "If she was considered immaterial, then why did Philips want an agent to keep an eye on her?"

"I asked myself the same question and started

45

digging for answers. Turns out that she really enhanced the bureau's AI capacity and then, with her brother's help, did the same when she went to work for Leo Montoya at Los Mejores. Leo has been on Philips's list since he became head of AITM."

"Why?"

"Because he specializes in AI and it's rumored that he sells the information to his clients."

Who are—?"

"Good guys with money, unlike anyone around the president or governor of this state. The whole point, Jake, is that you're now on the Philips radar and that may prove to be a threat to you, your ex, your daughters."

"Those threats are history, Max, you know that. You were there when they were happening."

"Philips wasn't head of AITM then. He doesn't give a shit about anything or anyone but the president. His loyalty to the psycho is unwavering."

"So what do you think the Ochoa woman is onto?"

"I can't say."

"Can't because you don't know or won't

because…"

"Theories, that's what we have. But knowing Luna's ability and how she works, I suspect what she has is mind-blowing."

You got that right. Mind-blowing, tragic, heart shattering, terrifying. But Jake didn't say any of that. "I'll stay safe, Max. And I'll make sure my family is, too."

"You really think that's possible with this gang on your tail?"

"I'll be discrete. Now I know I'm being watched, I'll take precautions. I'm not going to risk putting my family in danger again. I can assure you of that Max."

"Good, Jake. That makes me feel a little calmer." He stood and suddenly hugged Jake.

Max's care for Kate and the kids was touching. Jake knew he always had felt close to all of them and they looked up to and valued his friendship too. "We're in choppy waters my friend. You take care, and if I can help in any way, holler."

"Thanks, Max. I appreciate your help and your honesty." Jake walked with him to the door. "What do you think Philips is actually up to? What docs *he* want to do with AI?" He seemed to consider the question carefully. His gaze dropped to the floor, then he raised his eyes to Jake's. "Where do you think this presidency is headed?"

"Autocracy, dictatorship, a government run by tech billionaires with the rest of humanity as their...serfs. Dystopian, in other words."

"That's dark, Jake, really dark. But probably accurate."

Once Max had left, Jake quickly made himself some breakfast - a grapefruit, English muffin, a bowl of cereal loaded with fresh fruit. As soon as he sat down to eat it, he started worrying about all this. He needed to get Kate and his daughters to move elsewhere and suspected he should do the same thing. If those images he'd seen of the AI's predictions actually came to pass, then it wasn't just his family that was at risk but all of humanity. Every living thing on the planet.

Did Max know that?

Did Philips?

He had to assume they knew or at least suspected as much.

He felt he should call Kate, warn her, but given what Max had told him, decided it might be safer contacting her on a burner phone. He had one in the glove compartment that he had used once with an informant to verify facts for the *Florida News.* That would do. But when he was in the car a few minutes later, the burner plugged in and charging, he knew that a warning would alarm her. Best to suggest something innocuous like getting together for lunch or breakfast.

Jake punched out her number, a FaceTime call. She answered on the second ring, a good sign. It meant she wasn't pissed at him and was working out of the house. Her face appeared on his screen, an extraordinarily pretty face with eyes the color of the Mediterranean, an expressive mouth, soft, blond hair that fell to her shoulders. "Hey, dude, what's up? Tired of writing about women's beauty products?"

He laughed. "AI is helping with that. You planning another wedding?"

"Three more. I was suddenly inundated."

"How about meeting for lunch tomorrow?"

"Yeah, sure, tomorrow's good." She paused. "You look…worried, Jake."

She'd always read him well. "Yeah, I am. The direction of things in this country sucks."

"Well, yeah. I can't listen to the news anymore. Too depressing."

"So where should we meet tomorrow?"

"How about the Cassadaga hotel?"

"Whythere?"
" They've got a great restaurant. And I'd like to get a reading."

"What kind of food?"

"Don't worry, Jake. There are plenty of vegan choices."

"Okay, is noon good?"

"Perfect."

"How're the girls?"

She smiled at that. "They're young ladies."

"Yeah, yeah, I know."

"Well, Liz has a date this weekend. New guy. And Nicki is already prepping for SATs. You sure you're okay?"

No, not sure at all. "This too shall pass, right?"

She laughed. It was what they'd often said to each other in tough times. "Definitely. See you tomorrow."

Minutes after they disconnected, he pulled into a parking spot in front of Los Mejores, alongside a huge moving van that men were loading up with furniture. He found Luna and Juan inside, taping up boxes for the movers to load.

"Hey, Jake, good to see you gain," Juan said, "And congrats on becoming our colleague!"

"Thanks. Anything I can help with here?" Luna shook her head. "Nope nearly done. You've got the address for the new office in Sanford, right?"

"Yes, Leo gave it to me."

"The underground place he mentioned?"

"Naw, very much above ground. But he said you're welcome to move into one of the houses he owns up there." She slipped a piece of paper from her pocket handed it to him. "That's the second address on the paper. He said he'll pay whatever the fee is for your broken lease. And there's no cost to live in the house."

His skepticism instantly kicked in. Generosity? Or was Leo buying his loyalty? "Wow. But what about you and Juan?"

Juan dismissed that with a wave of his hand. "We're safe. You've seen how remote Luna's home is. Mine's even worse. The places were purchased under other names. Even the presidential drones wouldn't be able to find us."

"You'd better think twice about that." Jake glanced at Luna. "I got a visit from your former boss, Max Oakland."

"Max?" She looked surprised.

"He's an old friend from my days at *Florida News.*" Then he proceeded to relate what Max had told him about the surveillance Philips had on Luna. "I couldn't tell what specifics Max has. But he knows your work is connected to AI and he said he believes what you've got now is big and that's why Philips has you and Leo under surveillance. Also, since the president signed that executive order about private citizens and AI, it puts all of us in jeopardy."

"He may just be targeting known computer experts," Juan said. "In the hopes that something turns up. Same MO as the president." Jake nodded, conceding the point. "But for Max to warn me like he did indicates the threat may be real."

"Probably is real," Luna added. "Max doesn't go out on a limb for just anyone." Just then, one of the burly men doing the heavy lifting hurried into the building. The name tag hanging around his neck said, MIKE. "Problem?" Juan asked.

Mike looked alarmed. "Uh, yeah. Some asshole is out here demanding entrance into the building. Jim, my partner, pulled a weapon on the guy and told him to scram until he has a search warrant."

Jake hurried over to the window and peered out. "Well, well. No surprise." He threw open the door and strode over to the same short, squat guy who had entered his ex's office that day a few years back. But this time, he was dressed entirely in black. "So you're back, the man in black again."

"Kessler. Now *this* is amusing." Up came his hands, patting the air, his short little fingers moving almost comically. "I've been sent to sweep up the garbage."

"Where's your search warrant?"

"Don't need one. You comply or else."

"I'd like to shoot this fucker," said Jim, his gun aimed at the little man in black.

"No need." Jake walked right up to little man, grabbed him by his skinny shoulders and roughly turned him around. "Best hurry back to your car and tell your boss to go fuck himself. But before you go...." Jake slipped the man's cell phone out of the back pocket of his jeans. "I'll take this." Then he shoved him forward. "Bye-bye, Mr. MIB."

"Hey, you can't take my phone." He spun around, his odd face contorted with anger, and thrust out his hand. "My phone, give me the phone." Jake gently pushed his arm down to his side. "Adios, dude. If Philips has something to say, tell him to come in person and say his piece."

The MIB glared at him, then raised his hand and shook his finger like a school marm scolding a student. "You're going to regret this, Jake Kessler."

Jake mimicked him. "And you, Mr. MIB, are going to regret it if you ever show your face around me again."

His arm dropped to his side and he marched off, up the street to a parked blue BMW. Before he pulled away, Jake got a snapshot of his license plate.

Once the MIB's car was out of sight, the others hurried out of the building. "We'd better finish up here ASAP," Mike said to Jim, and the two immediately went to work.

"Juan and I have our belongings. We're headed to Sanford to check out the new office."

"Did Leo say when the house is available?"

"Now," Luna replied. "That was my understanding."

"Then I'm going back to my place to start packing up for a move."

"It seemed like you knew that little weird fuck," remarked Juan.

"Several years ago, when I still worked for *Florida News*, he walked into my ex-wife's office and threatened her and I happened to be working in the back room."

Juan chuckled. "I imagine that didn't work out too well for him. Does he work for Philips? Or the president?"

"Probably both, but it doesn't matter. They're all clones from the same asshole."

Juan burst out laughing. "Yuck. Gross image."

Yeah, it was. "See you both this evening in Sanford."

He drove to UPS first to buy boxes for packing up his stuff and walked out of there with twenty pieces of heavy-duty cardboard that he could put together himself. They were of varying sizes and just about everything he owned now would fit inside. The apartment had come furnished and he'd gotten rid of a lot in the divorce. He could have the place cleaned out by the time he headed to Sanford.

FOUR

Their new office building was located in a quiet, tree-lined neighborhood off of Old Lake Mary Road, northeast of downtown Sanford. As soon as Luna saw the place, she liked it. The building itself looked like it had stood here for a long while and had been refurbished, the second story balcony rebuilt with mahogany, the front porch rebuilt and extended to the right. She grabbed her pack and her computer and got out of the car.

Mike and Jim's van was in the driveway and they emerged just as she started up the sidewalk. "Got stuff moved in," Mike said. You want to have a look first to see if the placement is okay?"

"No, thanks, we can move things around if we need to. Any trouble on the way here?" "Nope. Just the usual I-4 traffic."

"Better than a man in black making threats. I'm glad you were armed, Jim."

"Me, too," Jim said. "That little guy was creepy as hell."

"Even though I think this open carry law is dangerous, I understand why Leo recommended that at least one of us should carry a weapon," Mike remarked.

She tipped them each a twenty and thanked them for their diligence and patience. Then she trotted up the front steps. No keypad to get in. She was pleased to see a double lock on the door.

The living room was large, with a connected kitchen off to her left. The soft blue walls would work well for any images they might need to project. One wall, though, held an exquisite painting of a field with a Golden Retriever jumping to catch a Frisbee. Whoever had lived here before had considerable talent, she thought. She noticed that the windows had triple panes, triple locks, and were hurricane proof, basically unbreakable unless ferocious winds hurled a coconut or flying chair.

Luna wandered around the spacious apartment. The two rooms on the first floor, where their desks were already set up, had large windows that faced a spacious, fenced backyard with a pair of towering cypress trees and an acacia tree with tiny buds. By summer, those buds would be robust and colorful. She climbed the stairs to the second floor. Up here, one room had a desk, couch and chairs that came with the place and the second room was set up like a conference room, with a large table and six chairs in the center. Both upstairs rooms had printers and foldout couches.

She returned to the first floor, set up her computer on the dining room table and put the wireless printer on a side table. She wondered what had happened to Juan. Had he swung by his place first? Or gone grocery shopping? Or shopping for something else? It annoyed her that Leo had told them not to text. She went back outside to her car to start retrieving the boxes: office supplies, several changes of clothes, personal files, phone and computer chargers, a cooler that contained stuff from the fridge in the old office, and supplies from the pantry like coffee, pasta, canned goods, detergent, dishwasher tablets. She set one box after another on the porch until her car was empty.

She glanced at the houses on either side of her. The one on the right was smaller. The two cats on the porch, the basketball hoop in the yard, the two cars in the driveway, told her that a family lived there. The place on the left was a single story with two wings, a long, curving driveway with four cars parked there, a fenced yard. No pets around. But an LGBTQ flag was stuck in the ground along the driveway.

Good. Neighbors safe enough. It was probably why Leo had bought the place.

Before she finished carting the boxes into the house, Juan and Leo swung into the driveway and Jake was right behind them. Greetings all the way around, then the four of them hurried into the house loaded down with their own stuff. She felt their urgency.

"What happened?" she asked. "And where have you been, Juan? I thought you were going to follow me."

"I swung by my place first and...and that little shit...the man in black..." He sank into the closest chair, rubbed his hands over his face. He looked deeply shaken. "That little shit man in black returned with cops, broke into the house, and... arrested me."

"They kept him for two hours before they allowed him to call his attorney," Leo said. "Me."

It didn't surprise her that Leo was an attorney but why hadn't he revealed this before? "What was the charge?"

"Possession of massive AI data. He has 48 hours to turn it over to the government."

"Maybe we didn't move fast enough," she said.

"Our timing was excellent," Leo said. "In a pair of houses to the right are a dozen fired FBI agents who are there to protect this data - and us. To our left, where the flag is, we've got an entire trans community fired from their respective positions in government. Across the street are federal prosecutors who were fired or resigned when told to do something illegal, and even a couple of judges impeached out of vendettas. Next door to them are state and local police who have refused the federal government's dictate to stop people of color as possible illegal migrants and take them into custody. And in some of the other houses are fired IT professionals and hackers who are working with us."

"Okay, hold on." Luna held up her hands "Are you saying this entire neighborhood is filled with these…these kinds of rebels?"

Leo smiled. "Yes. I've been creating this neighborhood ever since before the president took office."

"Holy shit." Her eyes went to Jake. "Can you…write about this?"

"We don't want that kind of exposure right now," Leo said.

"I can certainly write about communities of like-minded individuals," Jake said. "Doing that now. An acquaintance at the *New York Times* offered me a job and she wants explosive political material. But like I told Leo and Juan, if I do this, my ex and daughters have got to be protected. So they're going to be living in this neighborhood, too, until this underground area Leo told us about is ready to take in people."

"They agreed to it?" she asked.

"Uh, no. Not yet. She and I were supposed to have lunch tomorrow, but I changed it to breakfast since the *Times* piece will be in the evening news, a special edition about how this administration has brought democracy to the brink of extinction."

Juan held up the large bag that had been in his lap since he'd claimed the couch. "Brought dinner. Maybe we should eat while we, uh, discuss all this."

"Discuss the death of democracy?" Luna exclaimed. "We don't need to *discuss* that. It's happening. What we need to discuss, is what the fuck can we do about it? Where's this underground place, Leo? How much do the…the refugees in this neighborhood know? What have you told them? What's your plan? I know some of it, but not the whole thing."

"I have possibilities," Leo said. "C'mon, let's eat."

Luna hurried into the kitchen, found plates and silverware and handed them to Jake when he hurried in to help. He passed them to Leo, who set the table, and Jake brought out a large bowl and platter. "Juan brought Cuban and Chinese."

"Horrors!" She waved her hands in the air. "DEI! We're breaking the president's executive orders that restaurants must close down if they serve foreign food."

Jake looked surprised. "Really? When did that become an executive order?"

"It hasn't yet," Luna said. "But watch, just watch."

* * * * *

Watch. Yeah, Jake was watching. Carefully.

When Leo had called him and told him what had happened with Juan, he had met him at the police station and witnessed the entire bureaucratic shit show. Jake had been relieved that the MIB dude wasn't there, but others like him had been in attendance, three local cops who apparently took orders from the governor. From Philips. From the president's office. They had released Juan when Leo snapped, *How much are you being paid to do this, gentlemen?* Leo had paid Juan's $10,000 bond and the three of them had left.

Now here they were, all their lives at a crossroad.

They helped themselves to the Cuban and Chinese food. At first, no one spoke. Then Leo broke the silence. "Just so you know, the front door is unlocked. I've invited some of our neighbors around here to listen in - by phone or in person. This concerns all of us." He held up his cell, indicating that it was connected to several other lines. "Have you ever heard of the Athenian model of democracy, Jake?" asked Leo.

"As in Athens in ancient Greece? The original model of democracy?"Leo nodded.

"Heard of it. All citizens had the right to participate in government, right?"

"Not exactly," Luna said. "Women were excluded. So were slaves and foreign residents."

"So it wasn't a true democracy," Juan said.

"Well, when we update that bit and use technology to bring everyone in, it will be," Leo said. Jake couldn't see how any of that was possible at this point. "According to the images of AI predictions, the autocratic course this country is on leads to the destruction of humanity." Luna leaned forward, her expression earnest. "Are you saying that the AI suggests there is something we can do to avoid it's predictions?"

"Yes," Leo responded, "but it's not something just we need to do. It's something all of us need to do. All of society."

"You mean become like Athens with DEI?" Jake enquired, almost sarcastically. Leo shot straight back at him. "Look. How do you think we got into this mess in the first place? One vote every four years. That's all the power the average citizen has. And the rest of it is hoarded by a small group of politicians, lobbyists and the billionaires who fund them. Think about it. It's inherently unstable. The guys at the top will always strive to keep a hold of what they have and the more technology advances, the more information we have, and the harder it is for them to do that."

"So the more they need to push us down," Luna remarked. Exactly. It only goes one way." A noise behind them prompted them to glance back. Maybe fifteen people entered the room, men and women, even some teens. Leo greeted them. "More coming in?"

"Through Zoom," replied a tall black woman. "Everyone is listening in. And we've all got cellphones. We felt it was safer. We don't want to attract the attention of any eyes in the sky."

When the other group arrived and crowded in the room, the woman shut the door, locked it, and they all crowded around the table. Only then did Leo continue.

"The system we've been using to govern ourselves will ultimately always end up in a full - fledged autocracy. Long before AI, the Greeks actually predicted this thousands of years ago."

"But autocracy isn't more stable," Juan chimed in. "I mean, look at what happened in Venezuela."

"Which is why the AI's exact prediction panned out this way. Autocracy means more suppression, more conflict and eventually total catastrophe. This is how species get wiped out again and again across time and space."

"Wait. Are you saying this has happened before, or in other places? On other… planets?" Jake wasn't sure he bought that conclusion, but it seemed to be what Leo was getting at.

"It's called the Great Filter theory." Leo explained. "A possible explanation to the Fermi Paradox – the observation that, while it should be very likely that the universe is teaming with extraterrestrial life, we never – or at least hardly ever – see it. They all reach a stage like this and then wipe themselves out."

"So it's inevitable?" Juan sounded forlorn, Jake

thought, and sympathized.

"Not if we change our trajectory. Not if our democracy deepens its roots. Not if we share power, instead of leaving the levers in the hands of a tiny cabal. If we become a real democracy, where ordinary people from every walk of life are involved, then a whole new predictive trajectory opens up."

"C'mon," Jake snapped. "Athens existed in - what? The third or fourth century BC? And wasn't the population just fifty or sixty thousand?"

"Fourth and fifth century," Luna said. "And the male population numbered between thirty thousand and sixty. And all of them – except women - could participate in the assemblies that voted on laws and policies and governed the city-state."

"I can see how that might work for sixty thousand people. But for millions?" Jake shook his head. "In today's political atmosphere?"

"I'm with Jake," said Juan. "In today's world, divisiveness rules."

Leo spoke up again. "Look, we've never really had a real democracy. Things are so divisive because no one's opinions matter that much. Politics is treated like a sport. But if we all had to join in the process of really making decisions about the country's future, issue by issue, then our collective mindset – the very way we talk to one another - would have to change."

"We'd be forced to grow up," remarked Luna.

Everyone fell quiet.

Then a teenager near the back, a Latina girl, spoke up "My mom got hauled off in our Miami neighborhood one morning. She's Venezuelan, married to my American dad, but doesn't have her green card yet. We don't know…where she is now." Her voice broke, tears coursed down her cheeks. "Nothing can be worse than this and where we're headed. We have to do something."

"What's your name?" Jake asked.

"Angela."

"We stick with first names," Leo said. "Just to be safe."

This elicited a call out of first names from others. Ripples of familiarity spread throughout the room. Jake sensed that many of the people here knew each other already since they'd been working on the same team. But for some this was something new.

Leo pressed on. "For the first time, technology allows us to connect up in large numbers. Sure, this has led to the spread of misinformation up till now, but that doesn't have to be the case if we develop and organize a platform for this purpose. It would need to start by sharing objective information with people about policies the government is proposing. Then it would ask people to have a say, share their opinions and make suggestions for change, based on factual evidence that was shared. They could get instant feedback about possible outcomes that flow from this or that idea, so we could engage in a back and forth, learning and educating themselves along the way. Then we would get a range of genuinely constructive proposals arising at the end of it. And all derived from the people – a mass participation."

"So, I guess this would kind of be a way to tap into a collective human intelligence?" Jake mused.

"Absolutely." Leo nodded enthusiastically. "We can use AI to harvest the millions of proposals that emerge from this massive process and then draw up common themes, locate areas of consensus and make concrete recommendations out of them. That way, everyone can get a chance to work on, scrutinize and amend government policy, before it's enacted. These then would get shared with lawmakers." Jake looked around the room, at the Zoom screens, noting the reactions in the crowd. Some looked pensive, others grinned knowingly. They had been working on the solution already.

"This way we can really hold legislators accountable – we can learn how much of the proposals derived from this mass engagement with their electors they actually voted for in Congress or enacted in the executive," Leo continued.

"I don't trust them to even do that." Juan spoke out.

"Sure, our system needs other reforms like campaign finance, redistricting and a range of things" Leo conceded. "But without continuous participation with the people alongside it in a system like this, it'll always revert back to where we are now. Politicians of all parties will try and skew things, one salami slice at a time, to their advantage, till we end back at square one. The only thing that can stop that is the public getting directly involved in that as well as every other policy that's scheduled for the floor of Congress. In short, my friends, this is how we take back control. It's how we put all our hands on the wheel this time and change the story."

"And survive." Luna interjected.

Jake noticed that more people were nodding now.

* * * * *

Luna wandered through the crowd, talking to this attorney, that computer genius, this fired federal employee, and she chatted with the teens. These people all struck her as deeply committed to the idea of a real democracy, where people participate regularly. They'd heard the rumors about the platform being developed by some of the teams already. But they worried about the ability of big tech to take it over and use it as a mechanism for their own twisted ambitions.

With her own expertise, Luna was able to reassure them with some ideas of her own. What they created would need to be nonprofit and have fully open sources. That way, there wouldn't be any secret development to avoid competition and anyone could see if it was even tampered with.

Also, they could make sure all the outputs and recommendations from the AI were traced back to the original inputs from the voters who engaged with it. Each one of them could be given their inputs on a file to keep for themselves, and print out too, so there would be solid evidence as to how every recommendation was arrived at. This could all then be audited at any time. A bit like the paper copies of every vote that was fed into voting machines.

She glanced at Leo. A broad smile spread across his face as he listened in from a nearby cluster of people. "Have they seen the images?" she asked him.

"No. Do you think they should?"

"Yes. We all need to know how high the stakes are."

He frowned and the crease between his eyes deepened. He glanced out at the crowd in the room that had spilled into the kitchen and hall. "Okay, let's do it."

It took her several minutes to set up the computer and get the images in place, then she signaled Leo and he nodded.

"If I can have your attention," Leo called, and the area went silent. "Luna is going to show you the latest AI prediction of our current trajectory."

She started the images but couldn't watch it and turned away. She, Juan and Jake stepped outside. Luna turned to Jake, "You think you can convince your ex to move into this neighborhood?"

"Maybe if I show her the images, but honestly, I don't know. I'm debating about driving to her place tonight, while my daughters are there, and pitching my case. I'd like my daughters to make their own choices."

"How old are they?" Juan asked.

"Liz is sixteen a junior in high school, and Nicki is seventeen, a senior who wants to major in some facet of the arts." Luna touched his arm. "Don't worry. They'll get it. Drive to their place now. Don't wait until breakfast, Jake. Make your pitch."

"You're right. Thanks, Luna. I'll be in touch."

"Wait, hold on. Did you get moved into the place Leo told you about?" "Never had the chance because of what happened to Juan." "Crash here when you get back. You've got your choice of couches."

He flashed a thumbs up and left.

* * * * *

The pleasant neighborhood in Deland where Kate lived with their two daughters was a contrast of homes - old and new, small and large. Those that were old and small tended to have been built in the fifties, when AC was provided by window units that protruded from under every window in the place. The new and large homes belonged to millennials who now flexed their financial muscle.

Kate's place didn't fit into any category. Built in the early 1970s, its 2500 square feet was built around a central open courtyard and featured three bedrooms with connecting bathrooms, a kitchen, living room and small family room. A fountain stood in the middle of the courtyard along with a long table and chairs, all surrounded by a dizzying amount of greenery and colorful flowers. And that's where he and his ex sat with their two daughters.

They listened to his argument about why they should move into the safe neighborhood and that it eventually would entail living in a secure, underground location. Liz and Nicki glanced at each other now and then but he couldn't read their expressions. "I've got a piece coming out in the *New York Times* within the next day, so there's a, uh, real urgency about this."

"An article in the *Times*?" Kate looked horrified. "Jesus, Jake. You're putting us all in jeopardy."

"No," he snapped. "It's this administration that has placed all of us in danger. I'm just hoping to help mitigate it." He brought out his phone, went to the images Luna had emailed him. He propped the phone up against a potted plant in the middle of the table so they could all see it. "These are the images of the AI's predictions about the planet and humanity unless something changes." He started the images and got up walked away from the table so he wouldn't have to watch it again.

For long minutes, no one spoke. They kept watching. Then Liz burst into tears rushed over to him. Jake put his arms around her, holding her close. "I... want to go...with you, Dad. I don't...want to die like that."

"How do you know that any of this is going to happen, Jake?" Kate demanded, and turned off his phone. "You believe it just because some AI is predicting it? What total..."

"I'm going with dad, too." Nicki bolted to her feet. "C'mon, Liz, let's go pack some stuff. How much should we pack, Dad?"

"Clothes, computers, pillows and blankets..."

"*What?*" Kate shouted. "No way are you two going with him into this...this insanity."

Nicki spun around. "It's insane *not* to go, Mom," she yelled. "Listen to the news for five minutes, get a handle about all the shit that's going on. You know it's coming. We see it every dat. AI or not."

Then she and Liz hurried out of the room and Kate just stood there, glaring at Jake. "Fuck this." She threw out her arms and walked off to the corner of the courtyard to be alone. Jake let her be and watched his daughters scuttle off into their bedrooms. He marveled at their single-mindedness as he walked the corridors, watching each of them starting to pack. Then he returned to the courtyard. Kate stopped crying as he approached her.

"Who else is in this little community?" she asked softly.

"Fired federal employees - FBI agents, prosecutors, IT people, there are several hundred...."

"Where's this underground refuge?"

"No idea."

"Great. Christ. I'm going to start loading up the van. Should I pack food?"

"Just a cooler. I'll do it. Go pack whatever you think you'll need for at least a couple of weeks." "Weeks," she said softly. "But what about my business, their classes..."

"Don't you get it, Kate? My God, how much clearer does this have to be?" "I...I..." Her eyes flooded with tears and she turned and headed toward the house. Jake found a cooler in the garage, carried it into the kitchen and began removing stuff from the fridge and the freezer. The knot in his gut tightened.

PART TWO

Community

"Never doubt that a small group of thoughtful, committed citizens can change the world. Indeed, it's the only thing that ever has."

Margaret Mead

FIVE

Kevin Philips read the *New York Times* religiously every day, the best way to keep up with the liberal agenda. But when he opened the website that morning, the headline screamed:

AI Predicts the End of Humanity & of Life on Earth

AI has been called many things, but I don't think it has ever been referred to as precognitive. Yet, given the heinous policies of this administration and the corruption inside it, the AI predictions about the end of humanity and of life on this planet are certainly possible.

The country has pulled out of every climate accord with other countries; has cancelled NOAA, the agency that keeps track of local daily weather forecasts as well as violent weather like hurricanes; privatized social security before the stock market crashed; has fired tens of thousands of federal employee; abolished Medicaid, ending health care for millions; has deported half a million migrants without due process; arrested judges and state officials who have acted against the administration; closed the

Department of Education; stripped federal funding from universities; made vaccines illegal... well, you get the idea. The administration is gutting the federal government from the inside out and people are suffering.

If you don't believe me, then Google it and do that before they shut down the Internet.

The courts have tried to block some of this administration's actions, but the president now ignores the Constitution and laws, and 'overrules' the courts. He believes he's king, but the better word, I think, is dictator. That isn't just his aspiration, it's what he rapidly is becoming. The organization behind this brutally honest version of AI will be broadcasting images of the predictions very soon, so stay tuned.

by Jake Kessler

Kessler? When had the *Times* hired *him?* And why? "Shit." Kessler meant trouble.

He quickly went through his computer looking for the man's home address. Some dipshit address on the outskirts of Orlando, an apartment building. A few years back, before he'd gotten fired from the *Florida News,* he'd lived in an expensive home with his wife and kids. But he'd heard they'd gotten divorced and had sold the place.

Yesterday, he'd gotten a report from his best mole, the guy who said Kessler called him "the man in black - the MIB" - whose real name was Moe Bell, with a recording of their altercation outside the offices of Los Mejores, Leo Montoya's illegal AI business. Later, Moe had gone to Juan Ochoa's home with several agents and arrested him. Montoya and Kessler had bailed him out - and then seemingly vanished. Until this piece in the *Times.*   Just as he started to punch out Moe's number, his cell rang and before he answered it, another call came through and another and another. He guessed his people were just now reading the *Times* piece. He finished punching out Moe's number and - not surprising - he answered immediately.

"Yeah, boss, I just saw that *Times* article."

"I want in. We're going to raid Kessler's apartment."

"I don't know if he's even there, boss. He's gone underground, that's my best guess."

"We'll start with his apartment, tear the place apart until we find leads."

"How soon can you get here?"

"I'm already in Orlando. Where should I meet you?"

Moe rattled off an address and Philips quickly entered it into his GPS. "You're 25 miles from me. I'll be there within an hour."

"Perfect. My guys are all local," Moe replied. "Come in your gear, we'll have it videotaped. If Kessler isn't there, we'll make it look like we got him."

"See you soon."

Philips got up from the desk in his Orlando condo and made his way quietly into the spare bedroom. He didn't want to wake his wife, Olivia, at this hour. It was barely 7 a.m. The bedroom closet held his riot gear, weapons, special boots and vests, all remnants of his time in ICE. A year spent enforcing the administration's brutal immigration policies had taught him one thing: lies, repeated often enough, became believed as the truth.

He'd seen it firsthand – how people had been led to believe that immigrants were violent criminals flooding the borders when, in reality, only a handful crossed each day, mostly women and children fleeing horrors beyond comprehension. But he'd never voiced that truth. His job was to follow orders. It was how you won favor in this administration

Officially, he was head of the Domestic Terrorism Unit, a title that gave him nearly limitless power. And with this president, *wider was better.*

It gave him a lot of freedom to call his own shots, to come and go pretty much as he pleased. His salary enabled him to live in two places - D.C. and in Orlando, not far from Deland, where his son attended Stetson University and was majoring in political science and government.

He strapped on his gear, and selected his SIG-Sauer P320 pistol, and his trusted M4 carbine. He secured extra ammo and slung the rifle over his shoulder before heading to the door. There were other assault rifles that would intimidate. But this one had been developed in the U.S. in 1980, had been adopted for use in more than 60 countries, and he liked the feel of the thing, its accuracy. He included extra ammo for both weapons.

He barely made it into the hallways before Olivia appeared in her nightgown, rubbing sleep for her eyes. "What the fuck, Kevin. It's barely seven a.m, You look like a time traveler headed for Vietnam."

If nothing else, the remark branded her as what she was - a sci-fi novelist. "I do?"

She burst out laughing. "Uh, yeah. No AK47 or M11, no M1 carbine or Colt. Nope. You've got full auto capabilities with that M4. Who the hell are you after today? More moms and kids? Naw, naw, lemme guess. That Leo guy who made you look like an idiot?"

His silence was answer enough.

"That's it!" She pointed a finger at him. "You're pissed because someone outsmarted you."

"Shut up, Olivia."

"No, you shut up. Your boss is a paranoid, racist man-child who's gutting his country for his own gain. And you pretend you don't see it."

He pushed past her, heading for the door.

She shouted, "The guy you work for is a messed up human being who's terrified of anyone who isn't a white guy. He's also a climate change denier who figures that by eliminating the Department of Education and censoring books he can dumb down the population enough so they'll believe any bullshit he feeds them."

He ignored her and kept walking.

He got caught in rush hour traffic, but still managed to make it to the address that Moe had given him within an hour. It was a public parking garage and Moe was already there with half a dozen armed men in riot gear who were in a dark van. "We're just two miles from Kessler's apartment, Kevin. Follow me."

"Lead the way, Moe."

A few minutes later, they pulled up in front of the apartment building, car doors flew open, and the six men, Moe, and Jake all leaped out and headed up the sidewalk. A woman was out front with her dog, a Doberman that started barking ferociously and jerking hard on its leash to get to them. "Get that mutt back or I'll shoot it," Moe snapped.

She clung to the dog, eyes wide with fear, and retreated into the shadows. Philips ignored her.

They entered the building, short little Moe in the lead. He motioned them up the stairs, to the second floor, and Philips guessed the green light in the center of Moe's helmet belonged to a video cam, recording it all. They stopped at apartment 13. One of his burly men slammed into the door and it swung open easily. Unlocked.

No photos, no personal belongings, nothing but empty furniture. Inside, it was clear. Kessler was gone. Philips pulled off his helmet. "No video, no arrest. What now, Moe?"

A voice from the open door interrupted. "Excuse me. What's going on? I'm the building supervisor." Philips turned to find an older man, balding, with a white mustache, and a beer belly. "I'm Kevin Philips, the head of the Domestic Terrorism Unit. When did Mr. Kessler move out?"

"I didn't realize that he'd moved until just now."

"Did he pay you what remained on his lease?"

"He was doing month to month."

"Did he give you any notice at all?"
"No, nothing."

"Did he leave you a forwarding address?"

"Nope."

"Do you have any idea where he may have gone? Moved?"

"I sure don't. Is he a, uh, terrorist?"

"Suspected," Philips said. "Would any of his neighbors have any idea where he might have gone? Did he have any close contacts?"

The man hesitated. "He was friendly with Caroline, who lives downstairs. I can call her, ask her to come up here."

"Thanks, I appreciate it."

He got out his phone, texted. "Okay, she's on her

way."

Moe and the other men removed their helmets, relaxed against the walls outside the apartment, scrolled through their phones. Minutes later Caroline appeared at the top of the stairs. The same woman who had been outside with the Doberman that Moe had threatened to shoot. She looked at them, her gaze locked on Moe. "You," she snapped. "Little guy who threatened to shoot my dog."

Moe crossed his arms. "Lady, you were the one who sicced Cujo on us."

"*Cujo* was protecting me, you ass." Philips intervened. "Look, I apologize for frightening you. We're looking for Jake Kessler. Do you know where he went?"

"Nope. Try his ex-wife."

She immediately turned around and headed back to the stairs. Philips was already on his phone, tapping into the federal database for her name. *Kate Kessler.* She turned up at an address in Deltona, a town less than 10 miles south of Cassadaga, a Spiritualist community where just about everyone spoke to the dead. A town of psychic weirdos. Philips entered the address in his GPS. She lived 32 minutes from here. "Next stop, guys. Mrs. Kessler's home in Deltona."

* * * * *

At 4:30 that afternoon, Luna was in the kitchen, prepping dinner for herself, Juan, Leo, and a couple of their neighbors. She glanced through the window and saw Jake's car pull into the driveway. An attractive blond got out dressed in knee-length jeans and a red tee and sandals. The ex.

His two daughters, one a blond, the other a brunette, got out with packs slung over their shoulders and the four of them went to the back of the SUV and retrieved more packs and a couple of suitcases and boxes. They looked like they would be here for a while.

Luna hurried to the front door, opened it. "Hey, you all, welcome. Let me help you with all that stuff." She went to the blond, who was struggling with everything she carried. "I'm Luna."

"Liz, I'm Liz. My sister is Nicki. Mom is Kate."

"Thanks, Liz. Juan, my brother, is the guy coming toward us. The other guy is Leo. There's plenty of room for you all here."

Once they'd moved everything out of the car and into the house, Leo and Jake took them upstairs to get settled and Luna returned to the kitchen, to enhance her dinner preps to feed another four people. Jake joined her in the kitchen a short while later, everything about him urgent. "You've gotta see this, Luna. It's from the security cam in my apartment hallway and then from the cam in my apartment that I forgot to remove when I packed up."

He started the first video and she watched an armed group in riot gear move up the sidewalk, past a cowering woman with her arms around a Doberman, probably her dog. They entered the building and climbed the stairs to apartment 13. One of them slammed his body against the door…

In the second video, the commandos were inside the apartment, checking every room and closet and bathroom. No sound. Then the woman who had been cowering outside with her dog showed up at the top of the stairs. Philips obviously grilled her and she apparently got pissed off and they briefly had sound: "We're acquaintances. And no, I don't know where Jake went. Ask his ex-wife."

"I'm glad they consented to coming here, Jake," said Luna.

"Me, too, but it may not be enough. We may need…"

"Jesus God, Jake, look at this." Kate, his ex, now suddenly appeared and hurried over to them with her phone clutched in her hand. "My security cam…"

She tapped something on her phone and a movie unfolded that Luna watched with mounting horror. Thirteen people in riot gear, heavily armed, entered Kate's home and moved through it tearing everything apart - kitchen cabinets, the fridge, pantry, bedrooms, closets, bathrooms, utility room, garage... One of the men eventually held up his arm, an apparent signal to stop and desist because the place was obviously empty. But the men continue to search night stands, bureaus, desk drawers, file cabinets, digging through whatever they tackled, setting one article after another on the dining room table.

"I mean, what the fuck, they're acting like Hitler's SS," Kate burst out. "Yeah," Luna agreed. "And that's pretty much who they are. The president's SS. And very proud of it."

"I hope you didn't leave anything around that revealed where we are," Jake said. Kate looked irritated. "When this was happening, Jake, we were on our way here. Any chance these people know about this...this neighborhood?"

"Not yet," Leo said, joining them. "Right now, this neighborhood is just one of many that's traumatized. We're far enough outside of Orlando so that scrutiny of this area won't happen for a couple of weeks."

"You don't know that for sure," Kate snapped.

Luna realized that Leo looked surprised by that. "You're right, Kate. I don't know that for a fact. I shouldn't assume anything. I've asked my team to speed up preparations on the underground place."

"Where is it?" Luna asked for what seemed like the umpteenth time.

"Under Disney World," he replied.

" *What?*" Kate balked. "*Disney World?*"

"Utilidors. It's a series of underground tunnels built in 1967 by some engineers so cast members could get to where they were going without having to go through the different areas above ground. It's also used to haul away waste, bring in supplies, for emergency personnel. My brother is in charge of the place now. It's absolutely massive."

"Is it going to accommodate..." Jake threw his arms out, a gesture that encompassed the entire neighborhood. "...the hundreds of refugees here, Leo?"

"Definitely. Many more, in fact. Thousands. There are gigantic rooms that used to be used for equipment of all sorts down there. Gary, my brother, and I have been stocking it with foods, supplies, and have been sectioning off parts of it for accommodations, a dining room, kitchen, the works."Luna struggled to wrap her head around the planning that had gone into this. How long had Leo and his brother been preparing these tunnels? "What about Disney employees? Do they know about this?"

"They know that a lot of reconstruction is going on in the tunnels, but only a few know why."

"How're you going to get several hundred people into the tunnels?" Kate asked

"After 10 p.m., when the park closes. Gary and I will take everyone in, small groups at a time."

Jake said, "This sounds dangerous, Leo. There will be hundreds of us under Disney World while the place is open to the public. Cast members will be passing through, workers hauling off trash, bringing in supplies...."

"Gary and I have prepared for that. Some of these people will be given uniforms so they can move freely through the various parks or help with taking out trash or bringing in supplies. Others will be given costumes that fit the various themes in the park so they wander around freely topside. It'll work out, Jake. I think we've got most of our bases covered. We plan to start taking groups into the tunnels in the next week or two."

Given the security cam video she just had seen,

Luna felt it should be sooner than that.

* * * * *

Around six the next morning, Jake left the house in his jogging clothes and went out into the neighborhood for a run. No one was out and about, the sun hadn't even risen yet. Here and there, street lamps cast a dim light, enough to run without tripping over something in the road. The morning air was cool, crisp, and cleared his fatigue from a restless night's sleep.

A part of him had wanted to slip into the room where Kate slept and ask her, bluntly, if there was any hope for a reconciliation. But he just couldn't bring himself to do it. He knew it would sound too much like a supplication. Besides, it had been two years and other than the fact that he missed his daughters terribly, he wasn't so sure he wanted to reconcile. Fundamentally, he and Kate were too different. He was no longer in love with her and knew the feeling was mutual. Their daughters were their bond.

If he was really honest with himself, he was attracted to Luna because her passions were like his own. But given their current situation, acting on that attraction would be absurd.

He'd gone about a mile when his cell vibrated in the pocket of his jacket. He slipped it out and glanced

91

at it. No I.D. but he recognized the number. Jake stopped and answered it. "Max, calling on your burner?"

"Goddamn straight. Your disappearance is going to bring about some terrible repercussions for you, Jake. Philips is going to order your bank account frozen and your ex-wife's. He also intends to put a hold on your credit cards. You gave him the slip and he's pulling out all the stops. If you can, remove your cash and close the account. He has sent out drones to look for you, Leo, your ex, all of you. I've been able to divert them way south for now, but not indefinitely."

"I removed most of my cash before this entire fiasco started. But what do you recommend for Kate? Where can she transfer her money?"

"The same place I transferred mine, an overseas bank." He laid out the specifics and Jake quickly made notes on his phone. "Look, I'm with hundreds of fired federal employees. When it gets too risky for you, Max, join us. We've got a plan."

"I definitely will. But I want to stay where I am for now and feed you info whenever I can."

"Look, I appreciate that, Max. But please, don't endanger yourself."

"I won't. He nearly lost his mind about your article in the *Times*. So did the president. So keep piling those on, Jake. It makes them both reckless."

"You sure this phone is safe? For talking and texting?"

"Yeah, it is."So Jake told him where the neighborhood was and the plan that Leo and his brother had concocted. "If you're ready in the next few days, let me know and into the tunnels you go."

"Thanks, Jake. I really appreciate this. Okay if I bring my two sons along too?"

"Absolutely."

"I'll be in touch."

They disconnected and when he glanced up, he saw Luna jogging toward him. She waved and he waited for her to catch up. The sky was lightening and he could see she wore jogging pants and a sweatshirt and bright orange running shoes. Her dark hair was pulled back into a ponytail that bounced as she ran. Her pace was fast and steady and he guessed she did this regularly.

"What's going on, Jake?" she asked as she reached him.

He told her about the call from Max. "Is your

money safe? And Juan's?" She chuckled. "What little of it we have, yeah. Leo has been paying us in cash."

"Is *his* cash safe?"

"Yeah. I think it's been safe since before he started planning this tunnel stuff with his brother."

"Is he a billionaire?"

"That's what I understand. But one of the good ones. I don't know what the fired employees and everyone else in this neighborhood have done with their money."

"Is Leo paying all these people?"

"For the most part, I think he offered them a refuge in exchange for their abilities, their talents, to get us through this."

"Is it possible to see these tunnels before we go there?"

"I asked Leo the same thing. He said he would try to arrange it."

"Have you met his brother?"

"Just once, when Juan and I moved into our old building. He gave us a bunch of free tickets to Disney."

"Can you press him about getting us into the

tunnels? I want to look around, make sure it's as secure as Leo claims."

"I did that last night. He promised to have an answer for me today. I'll hold him to it."

She nudged him with her elbow. "C'mon, let's go get some breakfast."

They started walking back toward the house and both of them glanced east as the sun peeked over the horizon. "Look at that, Jake. Breathtaking, isn't it?"

He feasted on it, the streaks of red shot through with pale yellow, soft orange, and the grand blue against which it appeared. "Even the president and all this shit that's happening can't spoil that kind of sunrise." "Exactly what I was about to say. Is that telepathy or synchronicity?" "According to Jung, telepathy and all aspects of the paranormal are part and parcel of synchronicity."

"Wow!" She glanced at him. "How'd you know that?" "I got a master's in Jungian psychology, and right after I got into the doctoral program, I realized I loved writing more."

"Lucky for the rest of us. I've loved Jung since a friend gave me the Wilhelm translation of the *I Ching*. I read that introduction by Jung and realized synchronicity had been zipping through my life forever."

"Give me an example," Jake said.

"Days before I got fired from the FBI, I opened my front door and found a dead black bird on the porch, right on the welcome mat." She paused. "I knew what it meant. That afternoon, Juan and I withdrew our cash from the bank, put it in a metal box, buried it in our backyard. But I knew this somehow would work out because a few minutes after I found that dead blackbird, I saw the most exquisite butterfly I've ever seen."

"Was it near the dead bird?"

"Just beyond it, flitting around some blooming flowers. Transformation, that's what butterflies are about. Leo hired me two days after I got fired and hired Juan by the end of that week. I know it might sound ridiculous, but here I am." She opened her arms. "Guided by a dead black bird, a butterfly, and synchronicity."

Jake was completely taken by the story. By her. He started to reach for her hand, to tell her how much he admired her for what she was doing, but suddenly, in the distance, flying at about 500 feet, he spotted what he felt certain were a pair of drones.

He grabbed her hand. "Drones!" And they ran

toward the nearest building, a small community center, and scrambled into the tall, leafy bushes along the side.

He and Luna stretched out on their bellies and crawled to where the bushes were thickest. He heard the drones now, a low hum, a buzzing. He rolled onto his back, parted the branches with his hand, and peered upward. Still at about 500 feet. "Call the..."

"Already texted them," she whispered. "Leo had them on radar, warned everyone beforehand." Jake squeezed his eyes shut and wondered if any of them would get out of this alive.

SIX

The drones frightened Luna. Suppose they were equipped with technology that could detect her and Jake squashed back under these bushes? Or technology that could peer through buildings? Or, even worse, suppose this technology could identify who they were?

She lost track of how long the drones buzzed along overhead- ten minutes, thirty, maybe longer. At one point, the larger drone swooped down lower, less than 500 feet, and Luna, nearly convinced this drone could hear them breathing, buried her head in her arms and barely took a breath.

When she couldn't hear them any longer, Luna inched forward on her belly, along the ground, and made her way under the bushes, branches scratching at her. When her head popped out, she twisted onto her back and scanned the sky.

"I think they're gone," Jake said quietly and she turned her head, surprised to see he was maybe a foot from her, also on his back.

"Are they gone or just hiding?"

Her cell buzzed, a text from Leo. *Drones no longer on radar.* She read it aloud and Jake crawled the rest of the way out, then grabbed hold of her hands and helped her out and away from the bushes. They both stood there for moments, brushing dirt off their clothes, scanning the sky. Then he grabbed her hand and they loped back toward the house. She was eager to see whatever Leo had on all this.

It was still early and this time, a few cars were backing out of garages, headed out of the neighborhood, toward the interstate. To work? Were these people part of Leo's community? Or were they just others who lived in this area, ordinary people with ordinary lives who worked and raised families and weren't harassed or threatened or fired by this administration?

As soon as they entered the house, Juan motioned for them to follow him. He was clearly excited and hurried into the utililty room. He opened a door next to the dryer and called, "They're here, Leo."

"Bring them down," Leo called back.

They followed him downstairs to a cellar that Luna hadn't known existed. Leo stood in the center of a circle of computers and faced a wall where images of the drones were projected. The images began when they first had come into sight, a pair of them, one larger than the other, just as she'd seen.

According to the numbers next to the image, both of them were flying at 510 feet. "Government?" Luna asked. "Of course. Blue drones," Leo replied. "They've met rigorous DOD standards and are designed for secure, government-sanctioned operations. It's a look-and-see operation, that's my guess."

"Shit, so they suspect we're in this area?" Juan asked.

"No telling," Leo said. "But we're moving our timeline up just to be safe. Gary can get us into the tunnels today, just the four of us. We'll have a look around, see how the area can be improved or changed to accommodate everyone in this neighborhood." "Fantastic," Luna exclaimed. "When do we leave?" "About an hour. He's going to have costumes or Disney garb for us to wear."

"What should we bring?" Jake asked.

"Burner phones and we make sure we have each other's numbers. Pay attention to the computer area Gary has set up for us. It's where we're going to broadcast the first AI stuff."

"So we should bring our computers?" Juan asked. Leo shook his head. "Not yet. This is our check-it-out trip. We have to be sure these tunnels are the right choice." Juan snorted. "Way I see it, the only other choice we have - all of us - is to leave the fucking country."

"How many people are in this neighborhood, Leo?" Jake asked. "As part of your group."

He thought a moment, consulted his phone. "As of an hour ago, we're at 352."

"And they're all going to fit?" Luna exclaimed.

"It's nine acres and so large that staff use golf carts to get around," he replied. "We'll all fit."

* * * * *

The FBI director, Pat Kumar, had ordered Philips to D.C. so here he was, waiting in a private room in the White House, where Kumar's assistant had told him to wait. He hated being here, knew what it was about, and felt certain that Kumar would grill him relentlessly about the drones.

Sure enough, when the FBI director entered the office twenty minutes after Philips had arrived, he snapped at his assistant to leave them alone, slammed the door and stood there, glaring at Philips. "*Drones*, Kevin? You know how many calls the Florida governor's office has gotten about those drones? *Thousands.* It has freaked the shit outta people. Now they're seeing drones everywhere."

"There were just two drones, Pat."

"Wrong, Kevin. There were dozens of them, fifty, seventy, along the coast and several hundred armed residents along the coast opened fire at these drones. They downed three of them, which crashed in the Atlantic. I had to order a special scuba unit into the ocean there to retrieve whatever pieces are left."

"I didn't order dozens into the air. I didn't steer them to any coast. I ordered *two* blues to check out the area around Orlando, north, south, west, and immediately east. I..."

"Who ordered the raid on Kessler's apartment? On his ex-wife's home? Jesus, Kevin. That prompted this entire rogue group to go into hiding, to go underground. You know what the fuck that might mean for us?" Philips stared at the man, at the way his features all squished together, creating a rather grotesque image of the FBI director. He was obsessed with conspiracy theories, unqualified for the job he held, for leadership of any kind, and the only reason he was in his job was because of his public worship of the president. The enemies list he had published in his cartoonish book practically had guaranteed him this position.

"The rogues went into hiding long before this," Philips snapped. "We've lost track of dozens of federal employees you and the president fired. Where are they? You have any idea? And what about missing IT people? Or the journalists whose papers, TV stations, podcasts you killed? Huh? You have any idea where they are? This Leo Montoya has taken all of them, in, I'm sure of it, and…"

"Okay, okay, Kevin. Calm down." Kumar patted the air with his short, stubby hands. He paced, kept tugging at his tie like he wanted to rip it off. He stood maybe six feet but right now he looked about half that, shoulders hunched, body seeming to be bent forward. "I agree we've got problems to deal with. We also still have a lot of work to do. But the immediate problem is simple. If you didn't order fifty or seventy drones to anywhere in Florida, then who the hell did? We need that answer first and it's your most pressing assignment right now, Kevin, got it?"

"But Pat, that isn't as important as finding out where these rogues are hiding. They're our most dangerous enemies, men and women with talents and abilities who have the knowledge and expertise to overthrow your administration."

Kumar marched over to where Philips was sitting, placed a hand on either side of his chair, and leaned in so close Philips could smell his sour breath. "If you want to remain in this administration, Kevin, then you don't question my decisions or those of the president. You find answers." Philips turned his head and his hands flew up against Kumar's chest and he pushed. "Get out of my goddamn face," he hissed.

Kumar stumbled back, Philips bolted to his feet, and when he regained his balance, he spoke quietly, sharply. "If you do that again, I'll have you deported back to whatever European hellhole you came from."

"I doubt it. I was born in Miami. So I guess you'd have to charge me with attempted murder or some fucking thing."

For a full minute Kumar said nothing. Those dark eyes stayed glued to Philips, unblinking, perhaps unseeing, he couldn't tell. It occurred to him that Kumar might be having a stroke and Philips started to shout for help, but he suddenly blinked and burst out laughing. "Shit, Kevin. I think you've done a great job. Keep doing what you're doing. Find these rogues. Find out who ordered those drones to the east coast of Florida. When you have a name, the person will be the first to stand up against the firing squad I've created for anyone who engages in treasonous or traitorous acts and that includes ex-government employees and contractors."

The abrupt change in the man's attitude, his voice, his entire demeanor shifting so dramatically and rapidly that Philips didn't know how to respond, what to say. Should he laugh? Go all friendly and personable? Or just pull out his gun and shoot the fucker?

Except that he didn't have his weapon. He'd left it in his car because otherwise it would have been confiscated when he'd entered this building. "When did the president sign that firing squad order?"

"Today." He made an impatient gesture with his arm. "He has so many executive orders piled on his desk, just waiting for his signature, that I can't even remember what they are."

"Then who created them?"

"The VP, the speaker of the house, the head of the senate, a bunch of different people on the president's team. *Our team.* It's our time, Kevin. This idea of a government by the people and for the people just hasn't worked out. There's tremendous waste in our government and we're cutting it back or cutting it out altogether." He went over to his desk, jerked open a drawer and withdrew a long, fat cigar that he lit, puffed on. "Why should the taxpayers foot the bill for chemo treatments for some kid in Idaho who has brain cancer? Why should the people have to pay for everyone else's mother or grandfather in a nursing home? These social programs are all just John Gotti schemes."

Now *that* pissed off Philips. His grandmother had spent a decade in an Alzheimer's unit that his family wouldn't have been able to afford without her Social Security, and Medicaid later on when her condition had worsened. He remembered those distressing years, his parents sitting at the kitchen, piles of paper - bills - in front of them, then two of them arguing, yelling at each other, and his mother finally breaking down in tears arguing, *She's my mother. We have to do something.*

And so they had. One evening they'd taken Philips with them to visit his grandmother, who hadn't recognized any of them. He hadn't wanted to go, he hated the place where she was, it smelled of endings, of death. His grandmother had been stretched out in bed, an oxygen mask over her face, IV tubes leading into both of her arms. His mother had tried to rouse her, *Mom, hey, wake up, Kevin's here to see you...*

But her eyes had remained closed, her breathing irregular. Philips clearly remembered letting go of his grandmother's hand at one point and heading to the bathroom. The door hadn't closed all the way and through the opening, he saw his mother and father smother his grandmother with a spare blanket.

His horror had been so great that he slapped his hands over his mouth to stop the scream in the back of his throat and kicked the door shut. Then he'd turned on the water in the sink to cover the sounds of his sobs.

He was twelve at the time. He was now forty-two and in the past three decades, the vividness of this event hadn't dimmed or gone away. It hadn't left him. Sometimes, he dreamed about it, the dream so vivid he could smell the bathroom in that dismal place. He still hated his parents, now deceased, and knew this was his weakness when it came to the president and his ambitions. A part of him despised the president and his autocratic tactics.

"I think cutting social programs like this, Pat, is a big mistake. Voters are protesting all over the country. I know you don't like watching the news, but I think you should. You need to see some of these protests, what they're saying...."

"I don't give a shit about protesters. Neither does the president. In fact, pretty soon he's going to be signing an executive order that protesters will be arrested and charged with terrorism. After that, we'll start using them for target practice."

In other words, he'll be deleting the first amendment." Kumar was visibly agitated now, pacing impatiently, and made tearing motions with his hands. "The bill of rights needs to be torn up."

"That's up to Congress," Philips pointed out.

Kumar spun around. "Whose side are you on, Kevin?"

"Yours. I'm just pointing out what you're going to come up against."

"Maybe I need to make you my chief assistant."

No, thanks. "I'm better in the field, Pat. I'm going to find your answers then I'll be in touch. You told me earlier to keep doing what I'm doing. Find the rogues, find out who ordered those drones to the east coast of Florida. *Those* answers."

Kumar grinned and slung an arm around Philips's shoulders. "Thanks, Kevin. You'll do it, I know you will."

An urgent knock interrupted them and one of his staff hurried in.

Philips used the interruption to slip away. He hurried up the hall, eager to get away from the Kumar, that suffocating room, the conversation, all of it. He would find the goddamn answers he wanted but would hold that information tightly against himself until he was ready to release it - to someone.

* * * * *

Gary, Leo's brother, met them in the parking lot outside Disney World in a golf cart. Like Leo, he was tall, over six feet. Gray threaded through his dark hair and he wore jeans, a Disney tee-shirt, running shoes. Right in tune with the environment, Jake thought.

108

"Hop in, folks." He gestured at the cart. And as Jake, Luna, and Juan got into the back seat, he shook hands with each of them and introduced himself.

Leo swung into the front passenger seat. "Thanks for doing this, Gary."

"Hey, my pleasure. We may have some Disney people who want to join us. Cast members, engineers, plumbers, IT, all people with skills."

"Did you tell them what was going on?" Jake asked.

"Nope. They asked *me* what was going on. I told them to stay tuned."

"So you have costumes or uniforms for us?" Juan asked, leaning forward.

"Yes. And a map of the tunnels."

He flipped open the top on the storage area between him and Leo and brought out the maps. He handed one to Leo and Jake took the rest of them and passed one to Luna, Juan, and kept one for himself.

The Magic Kingdom tunnel map looked like an erratic circle that connected the various lands in the park - Fantasyland, Tomorrowland, Adventureland, Frontierland, and Main Street, the entrance. Among the various lands were restrooms, Liberty Square and other landmarks where cast members and employees could exit into the park. Jake realized this tunnel system was actually the first floor of Disney World and the park itself was the second floor.

"Do the board members or CEO have any idea what you're doing?" Jake asked.

Gary laughed. "Ha. I doubt if anyone on the board has any idea that underneath the park there's a whole other world that hums with activity and purpose."

The cart approached the gate and they were waved into the park. Jake hadn't been here since his daughters were kids. It shocked him that the place was so huge and boisterous, crowded with kids and their families, all of it set against the backdrop of these garish lands. Years back, when he and Kate had taken their daughters through Tomorrowland, he remembered thinking that none of this was how *he* imagined tomorrow. In all fairness to Walt Disney and his team, though, he couldn't have imagined his life now as tomorrow, either.

Gary drove the cart down a steep incline that twisted and turned and they reached a heavy metal door with a sign on it that read, *Employees Only*. He picked up a remote control from a cup holder on his right, pressed several buttons, and the door slid open. As soon as they entered the area, the door shut behind them.

They started through a wide corridor, past employees in costumes - Mickey Mouse, Cinderella, Goofy - past trash haulers, suppliers, and into a huge room. Here, he stopped, got out, shut and locked the door of this immense place, and motioned for them to get out and follow him.

He took them into a smaller room where all sorts of costumes hung from hooks on the walls, along with various components of a Disney uniform, if there was such a thing. Mostly Disney tees, shorts, jeans, sweatshirts, capes with blazing images on them of the characters that had made Disney as recognizable as breakfast.

"Find something that fits you," Gary said. "Then I'll give you the golf cart tour, throughout the nine acres of this tunnel, which should give you a solid idea about whether this will work for what, Leo? How many refugees?"

"My guess is nearly four hundred, including whoever you tap." Jake tried to imagine that, nearly 400 people wandering around in this strangely surreal place. "I'd like to see your computer area."

"That's where we're headed after you all choose your outfits."

Jake walked through this massive room and felt his childhood waiting around the corner of every costume, every tee-shirt. When he finally stopped in front of one particular costume, he could almost hear his grandmother's voice whispering to him: *I always felt sort of sorry for Goofy.*

Yeah, he had too.

So he became Goofy. Juan became Mickey Mouse. And Luna donned a Snow White costume. Leo looked the part of a Disney employee. In a sense, each of them became the physical archetype of their younger selves, the disguise that might get them through this. Had that been Walt Disney's intent in creating this theme park?

Well, if he ever had the chance to time travel, he would return to the era when Disney had moved into this area in Florida and ask him. *Hey, Walt, you know about Carl Jung? Sure, Jake. Met him on one of his trips to the U.S. Gave him a tour of the future Disney World. He told me it would succeed beyond my wildest and most hopeful dreams because it tapped into the collective unconscious.*

Jake could almost see this interaction between two older men whose visions had possessed such power that they'd manifested in the physical world. But maybe this was an ability that all visionaries possessed. Had Einstein understood the power of his theories on relativity? On space and time? Had physicist David Bohm understood the force and power of his theories on the implicate and the explicate?

Among women visionaries one of his favorites was Rachel Carson, the marine biologist and environmentalist whose groundbreaking book, *Silent Spring*, was credited as the catalyst for the modern environmental movement. His other favorite was Sally Ride, the first American woman to fly into space. There were others, both men and women, and he believed that the women of today would surpass Jung, Einstein, Bohm. But to do that, this president and his regressive policies needed to be retired, gone, vanished.

Once they'd donned their costumes, Gary nodded his approval and they boarded the cart again and began the tour of this vast tunnel system. Jake's doubts that the place wasn't large enough for an influx of several hundred refugees evaporated long before they reached the computer area.

As they neared Frontierland at the western section of the tunnels, Gary took an abrupt left and pulled up in front of what looked like the entrance to a motel. "This is the first floor of one of the Disney hotels, where we can accommodate a couple hundred people," Gary explained. "It was built originally for the engineers who designed and worked on these tunnels."

"Is there a dining area? Kitchen?" Juan asked. "Enough showers and bathrooms?"

"Yes to all. Want to look around?"

"Love to," Luna said.

"If it's not too much trouble," Jake added.

"Not at all. It's important that you all are certain whether the tunnels provide the safety you think we all need."

As they stepped inside the lobby, several workers greeted Gary, then he gave them a quick tour of the massive areas off of the lobby. There were a hundred and seventy rooms, doubles and triples that could accommodate families. Most had adjoining bathrooms, which led him to think that at some point this floor had been intended for guests.

"Well, folks?" Leo asked. "Will this work?" "It's ideal," Jake replied and glanced at Luna and Juan, who nodded in agreement.

"Great." Gary pumped his fist in the air. "Now, on to the computer area."

* * * * *

As the cart traveled along the tunnel from Frontierland, Luna noticed that a dog suddenly appeared from somewhere and kept pace with the cart. It was maybe fifty pounds, entirely black, white around its muzzle and a ring of white on its tail. "Where'd the pooch come from, Gary?"

"Oh, that's Nika." He stopped the cart and called to her. "C'mon, girl, hop in." Tail wagging, she jumped onto the floor in the back and greeted her, Juan, and Jake like long lost friends. Then Gary drove on.

"Who owns her?"

"No one. She got dropped off here a few years back when she was a pup and became the tunnel mascot. Everyone feeds her. She sometimes stays in my office, sometimes with different cast members. Her vaxxes are up to date, she has been fixed, she's a doll." Nika sat at Luna's feet, staring up at her, head cocked to one side as if she was trying to figure out how to greet Snow White. Luna leaned forward to love on her and the dog licked the tip of her nose in greeting. "May I adopt her?" "Of course."

Luna brought her arms around Nika's neck and kissed the top of her head. "Hear that, girl? You're now my dog."

Nika barked, her tail thumped the floor, and

Luna sensed she understood what had happened just now. Shortly before they reached Fantasyland, Gary hung a left into an area labeled SECURE. Nika jumped down from the cart and, tail wagging, bounded ahead of them to the double doors. Gary pressed something on his phone, the doors clicked and swung slowly open. Luna didn't know what, exactly, she'd been expecting, but knew it wasn't this. The room was massive, filled with computer work stations where half a dozen men and women worked. Nika barked and all six employees glanced around.

"Nika, girl, where've you been?" called one man, leaning forward, arms wide open.

Nika jumped up, her front paws landing on his thighs, and he brought out a treat and handed it to her. The dog took it gently then settled on the floor in the midst of the circle of computers.

Gary stopped the cart, they all got out. He quickly introduced the to the computer people. "We call them the Hacker Collective. The smartest tech minds in the world all jumped ship when their corporations all became collaborators for the regime. Their loss is our gain."

"Welcome, everyone," several of them called out. The man who had given Nika the treat, introduced himself as Ace and got to his feet. "C'mon, over here. We've got computers set up for you all, ready to go.

Let's take back this fucking country and put the people in charge for a change!"

"Leo briefed all of you?" Luna asked.

Paula, one of the three women in this computer crew, raised her hand. "He briefed us. I'm excited but also have a couple of questions. A lot of questions, actually."

"Ask away." Leo stepped forward.

"Well, you say that the source information on the platform comes from experts, right?"

"That's right – all the briefings on policy and the back and forth people engage in around their suggestions and what their implications might be. All of that needs to be derived from subject area experts and key writings in journals and relevant publications. It's a way of educating people on specific issues, which is part of the whole engagement process."

"In that case, how would this plan end up being any different from a technocracy, where the experts are the ones with all the power?" Ace asked.

"Good question." Leo looked around and Luna realized that as usual, he wanted everyone to hear the answer. "The experts will be the ones to advise, sure. But it's the people who will decide. Decisions are about judgements. We want individual people, from all backgrounds, to exercise their judgment and produce answers, through this iterative process. Diversity is key. We need broad representation from the rainbow of humanity, so we can benefit from everyone's lived experiences. That is where the creativity and innovation will come from – people from all walks of life regardless of backgrounds, ethnicity, religious beliefs."

"Just what this administration hates," Luna remarked.

Leo nodded. "Exactly. So, the facts from experts are the inputs that we feed into the process, but the outputs come from the people. The broadest possible array of people. In a technocracy, the experts are the ones who make all the decisions and have all the power. That's definitely not at all what we're talking about here."

"So the expert point of view is valuable," Juan said.

"Absolutely," Leo said. "Take climate change. This administration has fired all the climate experts, fired the NOAA employees, then realized they wouldn't have anyone who could provide hurricane and violent weather forecasts, unless the president got up there with his stupid Sharpie and pretended he knew what the hell he was doing."

That elicited laughter from the others in the room. That fiasco of the president with his Sharpie wrongly altering the path of a hurricane had been televised, Luna remembered, and apparently people in the room remembered it.

"The information the platform provides would need to be derived from scientists who are climate change experts. Otherwise, climate change denial could creep into some of the answers – which we know is completely contrary to the scientific consensus – and lead people to create recommendations for change that are actually damaging."

"We definitely wouldn't want that," asserted Luna.

"Exactly. It would defeat the whole object!" Leo echoed.

"Do the experts have a greater say on any of the decisions then?" Paula asked.

"No." Leo shook his head. "Everyone's suggestions count equally. It's modeled on Citizens Juries, which are themselves modeled on juries in courts of law. Expert witnesses provide evidence and then a jury of peers decides. If a jury hears conflicting evidence, then they have to weigh the different testimonies in the balance and discern their own truth for themselves."

"I love the idea of Citizen Juries," said Eamon, a redheaded man with an Irish accent. "I'm from Ireland and citizen juries are how Ireland managed to change its antiquated policies on abortion and to embrace LGBTQ rights. They held Citizen Juries, heard from people with lived experience and heard from experts in each area, too. Then they deliberated together and recommended changes to the law, which the parliament passed. They did the same with climate change legislation as well."

"Wow, that's awesome, Eamon," exclaimed Luna. "But Ireland has - what? Five or six million people? There are over three hundred million people in the U.S. who can vote."

"If the AI is as good as what we've got, then the population numbers don't matter," Leo said.

"Okay then," said Jake, whose interest was definitely rising by the minute. "Give us a taste of what you've got."

"Alright, let's head back to the neighborhood we call home for now and get it set up there," Leo said, rising to the challenge. "And let me tell you, ladies and gentlemen, you're about to step into the future."

SEVEN

Philips flew back to Orlando in a foul mood. He didn't feel like returning to the condo because Olivia would be there, of course, pounding away on her keyboard and wouldn't have anything pleasant to say to him. He had a small office downtown as well, but right now, he needed a café where other people would be but where he wouldn't be recognized. So Philips picked up his car at the airport and drove to a cafe downtown.

He found a parking spot on the street and went inside with the strap of his pack slung over his shoulder, his computer inside. He chose a table in the corner, away from other tables, made sure he had a WiFi signal, then went up the counter and ordered a cappuccino and a bite to eat. An egg and cheese sandwich on rye bread with a side of fruit.

He returned to his table, went online, and accessed the White House info on these drones - numbers, time launched, reason why, areas covered, and who gave the order. The initial order came from the prez's secretary of defense, in response to the request from Philips, and was directed to the area immediately to the north of Orlando. He apparently believed that Leo Montoya was operating there with Luna and Juan Ochoa and that Jake Kessler and his ex had taken refuge with Leo, wherever he was.

Those pair of drones had been launched at 6:23 this morning from a government airstrip in Orlando. About half an hour later, shortly before seven, several dozen more government drones had been launched from somewhere just north of Cape Canaveral. Launched by who or what? That bit of information wasn't noted. Those drones had been directed to the east coast around Daytona. Here, as the FBI director had been so quick to point out, hundreds of citizens had witnessed these drones, and many thought they were UFOs. Some of them had been armed and opened fire on the drones, downing three of them.

The special scuba diving team was in the water at 9:11 a.m., searching for whatever might remain of the drones. Interesting time, he thought. So the whole thing had happened in less than four hours.

"Kevin. This is a surprise."

Philips raised his head. There stood FBI Agent Max Osborne, the fed in charge of the Orlando bureau. He was in his early fifties, Philips figured, and had been in the FBI for probably twenty years, through five elections. When the president had started his purging of federal agencies, Philips had thought the long timers at most of the agencies would be fired first. That had held true for many of them - IRS, Social Security, Medicare and Medicaid, agencies that helped foreign countries... well, it was a long list. And the FBI and CIA long-timers weren't on that list.

"Max. So you escaped the initial purge."

"Somehow. I heard they were offering buyouts. I might've taken one. Except that I don't think anyone who signed up will ever get squat. That was just another lie. How come you're still working for him?"

"Good pay and I like the job."

"Yeah?" Max pulled out the chair across from Philips and sat down. He had a paper cup of coffee in his hand and set it on the table. "So as head of the domestic terrorism stuff, Kevin, who are the terrorists these days? Are there enough to keep you busy?"

"Protesters in hundreds of cities, daily. The president gets death threats and it appears that our secure computers have been hacked."

"Hacked for?" Max frowned and it changed the contours of his face so that he looked more formidable, more *masculine.*

"For our AI info, among other things."

Max sipped from the paper cup. "Oh, yeah, I read

Jake Kessler's piece in the *Times.* I didn't know he was writing for them."

"They should fire him," Philips snapped. "He's a hack who hates the president and his agenda to help this country, get it back on track. The president is trying to make sure people have enough money to buy food, insurance for their homes, health insurance, that they can send their kids to colleges that aren't infected with diversity."

He could have gone on and on, but the expression on Max Osborne's face silenced him. He looked like he'd swallowed several large rubber balls - eyes bulging, mouth half open like he might puke, one of his hands gripping the edge of the table. Then he exploded with laughter, his head thrown back, and while he was still laughing, he reached into his pack and brought out his iPad. He went online, tapped the keyboard, then turned the device toward Philips, so he could see it fully, completely.

Philips didn't have any idea who or what organization had pieced together all these clips, but they exposed the president for the autocrat he so desperately wanted to be. They seemed to reveal a man Philips had glimpsed frequently in the president's public bravado about his administration - that of a cowering inner kid who had been bullied and debased and ostracized by others. Once a bully had been created, he or she tended to be a bully for the rest of his or her life. He'd seen it in his own family - in his father, in his older sister.

Some of the clips of the president were embarrassing. The guy didn't seem to understand why or how some of the firings he'd authorized in federal agencies put certain populations at risk. Kids, especially poor kids, and malnourished kids in foreign countries. He seemed to lack a basic grasp of geography - and of policy. And any iota of compassion was conspicuously absent in everything he'd done.

He finally turned the iPad back toward Max. "I get it, Max. He can be a real asshole."

"No, he *is* a real asshole. There's a difference."

"You know about those dozens of government drones sighted over the Daytona Beach area?" Philips asked.

"I heard they were UFOs and people got freaked and started shooting at them, took down three of them. That was the local coverage out of Daytona."

"Nope. They were government drones. Blues. Kumar dispatched a special scuba diving team to retrieve whatever was left of them."

"So the president ordered the launch?"

"Unknown."

Max finished his coffee. "Well, back to work for me. If there's anything I can help you with, Kevin, just holler." "You know computers, Max. Do you think you can find out who launched those dozens of drones?" "I can give it a try. You have an approximate time for the launches?"

Philips consulted his phone. "A pair of drones were launched at 6:23 a.m. this morning and the target was the area north of Orlando. I ordered that launch. At 6:57 a.m., dozens of drones were launched from somewhere near Cape Canaveral and those are the ones sighted around Daytona Beach. I didn't order that one. Neither did Kumar or the president."

"Okay, I'll see what I can find, Kevin."

"Thanks, I appreciate the help."

"I'll be in touch."

* * * * *

Since the six Disney employees intended to join Leo's community, Luna picked them up after they got off of work and took them to the neighborhood to watch the new democracy platform demonstration. The idea was that everyone involved would download an app and security code Leo had created and use it to connect to this interaction. This way, the 300 plus people in this neighborhood could stay inside and participate just in case more drones would be out searching.

Luna wasn't sure what to expect from this demonstration. She didn't know what Leo had compiled. But he and his brother and Jake set up a viewing area in the living room where the images and interaction would be projected onto the pale wall. It would also appear on people's devices once they'd downloaded the app.

When everyone was seated, Luna counted 27 adults and six teenagers of various ages in and around the room, all with their cell phones and other devices ready. They spilled over into the kitchen and dining room and even onto the floor. The rest of the 300 were on their devices in homes across the neighborhood.

Leo glanced around. "All right, let's get started," he said, and turned on the projector.

"Hello, my name is Athenia. I see that your community is new. What are the most important initiatives and policies to run and govern your community? It's up to you. If you make some suggestions, I can help you draw them up." People looked at each other for a moment or two then, one after another, they began to type.

Suddenly the screen of her iPad lit up with an array of light bulb icons flashing across it as Athenia explained what each one represented:

"Jenny is developing an idea."

"Hannah is developing an idea."

"Geoff is developing a protocol."

"The people in room four are working on an initiative together."

Luna liked seeing how the numbers added up: ten, twenty, fifty people. As people added their input on their devices, Athenia then responded with feedback. This enabled each person to enter a back and forth to learn, deepen and perfect their ideas. Luna looked around and saw that everyone was engaged, their typing speed increasing, reading what came back more and more attentively, thinking a moment then typing again.

It went on like this for three hours. Luna was impressed by what she witnessed. Some people paced as they worked, others sat down and made some tea as they contemplated and returned. People were getting hooked. Then once each idea was worked through, Athenia would place the finished proposal onto the screen so everyone could see it. "Let's put this to the whole community," she would declare.

And so she did. One after another.

The ideas were broad, encompassing a wide range of areas concerning their future communal lives. Ideas about where to secure food, how to protect themselves from the administration. One of Jake's daughters suggested a place where the teens could hang out, several mothers suggested a playground area for smaller kids, two men proposed a rotation of lookout duties. Others suggested game nights, book clubs, competitive sports, self-defense and martial arts training for all ages, the basics of a constitution, how to resolve disputes, even how to create and circulate their own currency. Each idea was fully developed and thought through in a dialogue between Athenia and a member of the community before being presented to the others.

Once all these dialogues were finished, more and more people stopped typing and sat back. Hope filled Luna, an emotion that had been absent in her life for a long time. People relaxed in a sense of accomplishment. They looked at their screens and marveled at the comprehensive set of sensible proposals that had emerged from members across the entire community – all ages and backgrounds. Where ideas differed on the same issue – or even directly opposed one another – Athenia went to work again. The AI started to redraft and merge different proposals, as well as clumping others together in a way that was designed to spot patterns, find common ground and maximize consensus.

As the final list took shape, Leo remarked, "It would have taken me and my team weeks to have come up with this. Maybe months."

Now Athenia spoke again. "And now it's time to for you to vote and decide your final priorities."

Luna noticed that people's faces turned serious again as they studied the detail of each suggestion with a laser-like focus. Then they began to vote on them. As they did, the list of proposals on the screen started to shift as some went up the list and others came down.

Once again, Luna watched people's expressions, the growing excitement as they realized the list they were looking at closely matched their own priorities.

Right at the top of the list was a simple statement: *Keep fighting for our freedom.* Under it were three subheadings:

1. *We make all key decisions in this community together this way from now on.*

2. *We work with the media to describe and broadcast Athenia.*

3. *We recruit growing numbers of people and show*

131

them a better way.

Leo suggested they take a short break and suddenly everyone was standing, mingling, chattering away, moving around, engaged with each other. Luna made her way to Jake. "What do you think? she asked him.

"Really impressive. You?"

"Ditto. Leo really understands what he's doing."

"Even my daughters are involved. I love it."

"And your ex."

"Yeah, even her."

He surreptitiously reached for her hand, squeezed it.

Then his younger daughter hurried over and Jake released Luna's hand. She suddenly remembered Nika, and made her way through the crowd, looking for her dog. Luna had left her with a bowl of food in the kitchen, but she didn't see her. The bowl was still there on the floor, next to a large water bowl, and most of the food was gone.

She went down the closest hallway, peering into one room after another and finally found her in the bedroom where Luna had left her belongings. Nika was stretched out at the foot of the bed, asleep. Luna went over to her, crouched and pressed her face against Nika's soft fur. "I'm so glad you're here," she whispered.

Nika raised her head slightly, licked Luna's face, then her head dropped to the mattress again.

* * * * *

Jake's phone buzzed as he stood with his youngest daughter, Liz. He glanced at it. A text from Max. *Am in my car in a driveway outside the address you gave me. Can I come in?*

I'll be right out. Don't come out the front door, there's a drone nearby. Is there a back entrance? I'm toward the middle of the driveway. Stay put. I'll come out and motion you to a safe way in.

"Honey, a friend's outside. I'll be right back."

"Need help, Dad?"

Just then, his love for Liz flooded through him and he leaned forward and kissed her forehead. "No, no, keep your mom and Nicki company. If Athenia starts up again, get involved."

"I will. I already did. This is cool."

Jake moved through the crowd away from her

133

and headed for the cellar door. He'd been down here only once, surprised that a cellar existed at all. Yet, Orlando was 112 feet above sea level and he guessed this area north of the city was even higher. Even so, cellars weren't common in buildings in Florida.

He flicked on the switch at the top of the stairs and hurried down to the cellar. Four windows lined the far wall. There was also a door, just as he remembered. He went over to it, unlocked it, poked his head outside. Perfect. The door opened to a recessed area, with stairs that led up to the driveway. He slipped out, careful to leave the door slightly ajar, and went to the top step and peered out.

Max's SUV was less than five feet from him, headlights off, Max slumped down in the driver's seat. Jake texted him. *Am to your left, waving. See me?*

Jake waved.

See you.

Where's the drone? Jake asked.

Last saw it off to my right.

Did it follow you?

No. It's part of this ongoing surveillance. I left the bureau. Philips asked me to help him find the person responsible for the launch of dozens of gov't drones over the Daytona Beach area. They seem to have really spooked people in the area and it's going viral. Three went down in the Atlantic and some special retrieval team supposedly was dispatched to find the pieces. But shit, I was responsible for that launch. I did it to distract the pair of drones over your area. Sooner or later, he'll figure that out, so I'm not giving him that opportunity.

What did you do?

Made it look like Kumar launched those drones himself.

Holy shit. Could they still figure out it was you?

I covered my tracks well, but who knows. It's possible. I need to be careful

Christ almighty, yes you do. Ok. If you back up without headlights on, move next to the staircase here and then get out and get in here. You have bags?

Pack with clothes, my laptop.

Jake scanned the sky overhead but didn't see anything unusual. But that didn't necessarily mean they were in the clear. *Back up first, then set your pack on the ground outside the door, and I'll pull it in,*

135

Max backed up without headlights and parked so close to the entrance of the stairs that when he set his pack outside the door, Jake grabbed a nearby broom, hooked the handle under the pack's strap, and pulled it over. No shots were fired, no alarms went berserk.

Coming over to you now, Max texted.

The door opened again and Max literally crawled out of the car and scrambled on his hands and knees toward Jake. Once he was safely in the stairwell, Jake used the broom handle to shut Max's car door. "I'm glad you're here," Jake said.

Max sat on a lower step, hands covering his face. "These fuckers. They're really shattering anything we could ever have called democracy."

"It's probably because we never had a proper one to start with. It was always too shallow - vulnerable. You've got to see what's happening upstairs. The platform Leo designed is organizing a grass roots democracy. If we make it through this, then that's the kind of things we need to be doing in future."

"Great. Let's do it."

"I'm texting you the app to download."

"Got it." Max downloaded it as they climbed the stairs to the main floor. "Hope there's room for me here."

"Absolutely."

Jake and Max stood at the back of the crowd, in the kitchen doorway. "I'm calling for a vote now," Leo said. "If you agree with this list of initiatives and policy proposals, and in this order of priority, then raise your hand if you are in this room. Otherwise type a YES or NO on your screens."

YES was unanimous.

"Excellent" Leo exclaimed.

"Here are the key steps to implementing your first priority." Athenia spoke before listing the following:

We decide all key issues in this way together from now on:

1. From now on we will engage in a rolling dialogue on Athenia.

2. Any suggestion that aligns with this top priority list and is proposed, in one form or another, by more than 2% of the community, will be worked up and put to a vote by all.

3. We should have an Implementation Executive (IE) whose main job is just that. To implement what has been agreed only, and then make suggestions for change, if difficulties or issues arise.

4. Any suggestions from the IE will also need to be voted on by all.

We work with the media to describe and broadcast Athenia:

1. Get the word out about the truth of, not only of what this administration is doing, but how the calamitous trajectory we are on is inevitable with our current week and limited system of democracy. So through more articles in the Times and online.

2. Talk about platforms like Athenia and how there is another way we can organize ourselves as a society. Not just in a small community like this, but at larger scale too. It doesn't require huge or endless meetings or everyone to log on at the same time. It doesn't need to take over everyone's lives. A bit of attention each day from every person will mean we can all steer the ship of government together and abolish our personality driven, toxic and evidently lethal political culture for good.

We recruit growing numbers of people and show them a better way:

1. We need to start by weakening their surveillance and message monopoly by hacking government

computers to ground drones, planes, vehicles, and kill cell phones

2. Release Athenia's code on open source sites, for any community willing to use it

3. Have community defenses ready for any government backlash, with armed lookouts organized 24/7

4. Have plenty of food and supplies in place & make arrangements with local grocery stores to ensure food is available.

5. Check the water supply and ensure it is safe and plentiful

6. Gradually welcome new people into the community as they find us, with rigorous vetting and security checks for each

7. Plan for or a move to the underground facility when security concerns become too high for this neighborhood, which they inevitably will at a certain point

8. When safe, send ambassadors out from here to help nurture other similar communities that form around the country over time too

Utter silence in the house followed these lists, then everyone spoke at once. Leo once again held up his hand. "It's now nearly two a.m. Let's convene tomorrow and discuss the first steps then. Jake, since you've got a connection to the *Times*, how soon can you have something to submit – a follow up to your last piece?"

"As soon as you need it."

"If we have any other writers in the community, please get in touch with Jake so we can be prepared to take on social media, too."

Jake quickly texted Leo about Max. He glanced at his phone, flashed a thumbs up. "Any ex-law enforcement personal - federal, state, local - should get in touch with Max Osborne, ex-FBI as of a few hours ago. Max, can you raise your hand?"

He did so. "Your group will probably be the best equipped to handle these lookouts.

Any hacking and computer experts should get in touch with Luna and Juan Ochoa. They'll take you to meet our elite Hacker Collective in the computer center tomorrow. We'll also need people who are water experts to gather together a team to check on our water supply and we'll need people to negotiate with local grocery stores. All of this can be organized tomorrow. Think about it all tonight and we'll vote on a time frame in the morning. Questions?"

A few hands went up but Jake could see that people were tired. Jake elbowed Max. "C'mon, let me show you your room."

They headed for the stairs and once they got through the crowd, Max said, "I'm impressed, Jake. There's a real vibe here. I think there's hope."

"Same here. But let's see, right?"

EIGHT

L una had fallen into bed at three and Nika woke her four hours later, whining softly and licking her face. She had left the door to the porch open so that Nika could go out into the yard if she needed to go to the bathroom and suspected the dog had awakened her for some other reason.

"What is it, girl?" Luna drew her hand over Nika's head and back.

Nika barked. It sounded urgent.

"Okay, give me a minute." She swung her legs over the side of the bed, dressed quickly in jeans and a tee, hurried into the bathroom to brush her teeth and wash her face. When she turned to leave, Nika was waiting just outside the bathroom door for her, her tail thumping against the floor. Luna scooped up her phone. "Now show me what the issue is."

She barked again and ran out the open porch door. Luna followed her. The dog stopped on the porch, peered upward, and so did Luna. There, barely visible in the light of the rising sun, she spotted what looked like a drone. She guessed it was a mile high, which might explain why she didn't hear it. Or, it could be a silent drone. When she'd worked for the bureau, she'd heard that the Department of Defense was developing them but she'd never seen one.

She tucked her fingers under Nika's collar, urging her back into the shade under the awning, and texted Jake. *Silent drone about a mile above us.*

He surprised her by answering almost immediately. *Watching from window. You @ computer?*

No, on porch outside my room Nika alerted me to it, woke me up. Am going to computer center to see what I can find out.

Will meet u there.

Fortunately, she didn't have to leave the house to get to the computer center. It was still set up in the living room from the AI demo. She and Nika hurried downstairs and on their way up the hall, ran into Leo. "I was just about to wake you. There's a…"

"Silent drone," she said. "About a mile above us. Nika alerted me to it."

"Fantastic. Good dog, Nika." He stroked her head. "You have a permanent home here with us, you know."

In the computer room, Leo already had the radar

visible on the wall, the drone clearly visible and moving slowly from east to west. "Any idea about the capabilities of these things, Leo?"

"Nope. Let me see if my defense AI knows." He flipped open the lid of his iPad. "Neptune, what can you tell us about that silent drone up there?"

"Good morning. The silent drones are the DOD's newest tools."

"Neptune?" This was the first time Luna had heard of any device called Neptune.

"When I was originally working on Athenia, I developed several other AI devices. Neptune was designed to use government intelligence to develop defensive capabilities of its own to protect the community."

"Wow, Leo, you keep a lot to yourself," she remarked.

He smiled. "That's the nature of things."

"These drones are completely silent," Neptune added. "They can fly as high as 10,000 feet and have superior surveillance capabilities."

"Any way we can disable it?" Luna asked.

"I can," Neptune replied.

The drone appeared on the radar on their iPad screens.

"How're you going to do this?" Luna asked.

"I know how it was developed, where it's weak," Neptune replied.

"Fantastic," Leo said. "Do it. Disable it."

The drone remained on the radar screen until it was well beyond the Orlando area and approaching Ocala National Forest 70 miles to the north. Then, suddenly, the front of it dipped down and kept dipping until it plunged earthward.

"Done,"

"Where did it come down?" Luna asked.

Coordinates appeared on his screen and also on the wall. "It's in the thickest and wildest part of that national forest," Neptune said. "It will be difficult to find,"

"What did Neptune do exactly, Leo?" asked Luna.

"It changed a number in its code. There are four other silent drones the DOD developed."

"Four more. Shit," she spat. "But maybe until they figure out why this one went down, they won't launch any of the others."

"I will alert you if they do," Neptune said.

"Alert us how?" Luna asked.

"Your phones…"

Both phones made an odd, distinctive sound and Nika barked. "Great," Leo said.

Max joined them with three cups of coffee. He handed one to each of them, sipped from his own. Luna said, "Neptune, this is Max Osborne."

"Greetings, Max. Good that you joined us."

"Neptune just disabled a silent drone," Luna said.

Max laughed. "Kumar is really going to hate this. He believed those drones were invincible. He's probably dispatching a search team right now."

With the drone taken care of, Jake looked around as if to find his bearings then turned to the kitchen. "Right. I'll fix us breakfast," and headed toward the kitchen. Luna followed behind with Nika trotting alongside her.

* * * * *

Philips sat at the table in his Orlando kitchen,

working on the breakfast Olivia had made for them. Omelets, toast, hash browns. They both scrolled through their phones, the silence between them an impenetrable wall until she said, "So how was your little jaunt to Vietnam? Did you get the bad guys?"

"Very funny." Then he got up, barely resisting the urge to toss the rest of his coffee in her face. "I need to take a call."

"Call away, Kevin. Being a loyalist to this president means you'll go down with the rest of his staff when this admin is done."

He ignored her and went into his office, shut the door, locked it. The call that came through was from the president's chief of staff, Sarah Wells. "Kevin, you alone?"

"I am now. What's up, Sarah?"

"Our Nationwide Drone Surveillance Program – NDSP - it's under threat."

This had to be serious, Philips thought. The NDSP was a program no one ever referred to out loud. All autocratic regimes needed a secret police or at least they used to. But drone technology had rendered secret police obsolete. The president could station his eyes and ears literally everywhere. The roll out for this had been happening by stealth ever since the first weeks of the administration. They took the boil a frog approach. That meant a slow gradual build up towards a state where a drone would be in every corner, outside every building, looking into every household, observing everything, recording everything. And it was implemented so slowly and steadily that no one would much notice it happening. Even though they weren't supposed to believe in most of science, they recruited the best psychological and scientific minds to work on the design of the delicate incremental roll out, and no one was supposed to speak about it. Until now.

"NDSP? How is that possible, Sarah? It's just about the most secret program we have," Philips enquired.

"Those drones over the Daytona area yesterday. It was a sudden spike in drone activity and people began to notice. Now the media is all over it and people are seeing our drones everywhere. How could this have happened? Where did those ones in Daytona come from? Have you found out yet?"

"They definitely weren't ours? "Of course they weren't, Kevin! Why would we jeopardize our whole program by drawing attention to drones like that?"

"Yeah, I get it."

"I want you to find out who did it, Kevin. The

President told me to ask you to hurry up. He needed to know yesterday." "Okay." A reflexive answer. But where to start?Sarah answered without him asking. "Start north of Orlando. Something suspicious happened there and we think it might be linked."

"What happened?"

"Someone brought down one of our best drones there. Someone who clearly knows what they're doing."

"Where north?"

"Texting you the range of coordinates."

He entered the coordinates into the GPS. It covered a fairly large area – from Altamont Springs to Cassadaga. "How high was this drone?"

"About 10,000 feet."

"Was it shot down?"

"Our data shows that it was, uh, disabled. We don't know how."

AI? "Damn, Sarah. Send me the coordinates where it went down."

"It went down somewhere in the Ocala National Forest. But keep in mind that it was disabled before that and had to descend 10,000 feet, Kevin."

"Okay. I need some time to get a team together, then I'll move on out."

"Stay in touch."

"I will."

When they disconnected, Philips brought up a map of central Florida on his phone that showed the coordinates Sarah had given him. By air and on the ground, he thought, that would be the most efficient way to search.

He contacted his pilot, Chet, and two security personnel first. *Search & find job. Need a chopper to be eyes in the sky while my team & I are on the ground. We're going to start in the middle of the area to be covered. So meet me @ Million Air in Sanford in about an hour.*

So it's the Sanford area for search & find? Chet asked. *Initially, yes. What kind of gear do we need?* This question came from one of the security guys. *Usual weapons. High powered binocs. Change of clothes just in case it takes a while. Cooler with food & water.*

The second security man replied, *See you in an hour, Kevin.*

Now: his ground team. He wanted to have at least five others and knew exactly who to tap – men in the president's private army. The press had gotten wind of this private army, of course, but didn't have any proof. He immediately sent a group text and suggested they meet at his office in downtown Orlando. All five were available and agreed to meet in ASAP.

He didn't have to pack much. His gear and weapons were in the back seat of his car. He would pick up his team and the drive to the airstrip would take less than 30 minutes, if the morning traffic cooperated.

On his way out the front door, Olivia called, "Wake up, Kevin! You'll be the one who goes down, not the prez!"

In response, he slammed the door on his way out. She pissed him off. He didn't need or deserve that. After all, this might ingratiate him with the prez so that in his next term, who knows, maybe he could be secretary of state.

* * * * *

Jake stood with Max, Luna and Juan in the main room of the house, now officially the computer control room. It was noon and more than 300 community members were online. Leo reported the news and the progress so far on the various committees.

"Early this morning, a new AI system I recently developed, Neptune, disabled a silent drone - one of five the government developed - that was cruising through the skies overhead. It went down in the Ocala National Forest. We don't know if others will be launched to this area, but just remain vigilant and aware if you're outside. Neptune, could you show them what the radar caught of this silent drone?"

"Certainty," the AI replied. "I've enlarged the image."

The drone looked much larger than most of the drones Jake had seen and far more fortified for the altitude it could reach. Across the side in bright yellow was SD1.

Neptune spoke up. "These silent drones are armed with various weapons. The SD1 had small explosives onboard that may have been rendered useless when Leo disabled it."

"Have they found the remains?" Juan asked.

"Unknown."

"Where was the SD1 launched from?" Max asked.

"Jacksonville," Neptune replied.

The images vanished and in their place appeared

a TV news report from a march in New York, showing thousands of people marching, angry, shouting, but peaceful. "They want to watch us so they can control us." This came from one male protester who was interviewed.

Another protester, gripping a sign, added, "It's all part of the same plan – arresting people off the street, disappearing people off to foreign torture chambers – they want eyes on us day and night so they can swoop in anytime they want." A man behind barged forward, "And that piece in the New York Times about AI predicting the gruesome ending that we are all headed for. It's just horrifying, all of it."

"Eyes off! Hands off!" The crowd chanted over and over and the camera panned back to reveal block after block crowded with protestors, then a split screen emerged to show the same in city after city across the country.

"Traffic is being brought to a standstill across multiple cities today as the protests against the president's policies of surveillance and sequestration of American citizens appear to be spreading across the nation," said the presenter. "We're even seeing drivers leave their cars in traffic to join the protests."

The image on TV faded away and Leo spoke again. "Okay, this is a fire we need to fuel."

"Hell yes!" and cheers erupted around the room. Then he turned to business.

"Now let's hear from Jake, Max and the Ochoas about the progress of their particular groups. Jake?"

"I've got the second piece for the *Times* written and a separate piece for social media. We'll add more detail to the AI predictions and then introduce the alternative path. We just need to agree on a date when to release them."

"Okay, Max, have you got volunteers for the lookouts?"

"I do," Max replied, getting out his phone. "And I'd like to thank everyone who came forward to volunteer their time and expertise. Starting later this afternoon, the first group of five will station themselves around the neighborhood from four to midnight." He called out five individuals. "They will also put up video cameras that can be monitored by all the lookouts on their phones and by Neptune. Another five lookouts will work from midnight to eight a.m. and a third group will take the eight to five shift." He followed this announcement with the names of ten more community members. "I'll be moving around during each of these shifts in case anyone has a question or needs something. We also have a backup unit in the event anyone is ill or can't make their shift. Questions?"

A man wearing a blue baseball cap at the back raised his hand Suppose one of us spots a drone or something suspicious? Where or to whom do we report it? And will the lookouts be armed?"

"If anyone in the community spots a drone or something suspicious, contact me," Max said. "And Neptune. And yes, all lookouts will be armed. Shoot only to defend yourself or someone else."

"Is Neptune our weapon for high-flying drones that bullets can't reach?" A woman sat next to the previous questioner asked "Good question," Max said. "Yes, in such instances Neptune will be our weapon. Leo has access and so we'll need to approach him for activation."

Jake turned to Luna. "Where do things stand with the local grocery stores and supplies?"

"I don't know. Your ex and I are headed out there when we're done here."

"Kate came to you?"

"Yeah."

That shocked him, but he took it as a positive sign. "She does know a lot about food because she has planned so many weddings."

"As soon as Athenia has collated, I'll grab Kate

and we'll head over to the local grocery place. "I'm supposed to go with Max to his apartment so he can pick up more of this stuff."

Their fingers connected and they found themselves spontaneously holding hands again. Luna looked at him and smiled. It clearly meant something. He turned towards her so they were eye to eye. He touched her face as their lips edged closer. Then Leo spoke up, interrupting the nascent kiss.

"Around four this afternoon, I'd like to invite the entire community into the plaza to let our hair down a bit, come together celebrate our community, it's achievements and the new way we want to bring about."

"Wow," Luna whispered. "What an awesome idea."

The plaza was a beauty. There was a fountain in the middle with a gorgeous plume of water and it was surrounded by lush foliage – hibiscus bushes with brilliant yellow blooms, gardenias that scented the air, roses that burst with color. Scattered here and there were benches, even several hammocks. Ideal for a community gathering.

* * * * *

As Luna stepped onto the porch, she received a

text message from a former colleague at the bureau who was fired in the same wave of firings that she was. *Hey, girl, Izzy here. Check your whatsapp.Headed there now.*

She hung back as Jake hurried on ahead of her, into the room, and clicked on whatsapp.

Luna, we need to get together to talk, trade some resources. Since asshole took office, I've been creating an army of protesters. Inheritance from my aunt helps fund it. It's now over 2K strong and growing by the hour. People are pissed. Their liberty and rights are being jerked away from them and they're ready to fight for all that.

I know you're working for Leo Montoya, the dude the prez and his boys would like to see strung up. I think if we join forces, we can defeat these pricks. Lemme know what u think, girl.

Her heart slammed into an erratic tango. 2,000 people? A small army! Luna quickly tapped keys: *Can you meet me at Nick's Grocery, Orlando area, in about 30 minutes.*

I'll be there. Where r u now?Safe place, close enough, talk when we see each other. U?

Same. See you soon, girl.

Luna hoped WhatsApp was as secure and

encrypted as it claimed to be. She quickly found her brother on the app, then went looking for Leo, Jake, Max and several others who needed to know about this.

NINE

When the meeting was done, Luna texted Jake's ex-wife and they met up a few minutes later in the public parking lot where most of the community members left their cars if they didn't have a garage. As usual, she looked like she'd walked out of a fashion magazine. Her lightweight khaki slacks fit her exactly right, her short-sleeved blouse was a soft bluish pattern with a hummingbird on the pocket, and she wore a pair of Skechers. Comfortable, but stylish.

"So how're we approaching the owner of the market?" she asked when they were in Luna's car.

"As directly and honestly as possible."

"I collected a lot of cash from community members who need supplies. And a list of stuff everyone can use like eggs, bread, fruit, meats and so on. Jake's a vegan and there're at least another 50 or 60 in the community."

"I've got some cash, too," Luna said. "I don't have any idea how large this market is or what all they carry. So we may be doing business with more than one market. Also, I got a text from a former colleague at the FBI and she's got two thousand people on the same page we are. She's meeting me at the market." *Two thousand?* My God, where are all those people hiding?"

"I suspect they live all over this area, in their own homes and communities."

"Will they join us?" "Hope so." She looked over at Kate. "How bad was the harassment against your family when Jake worked at the *Times* during this administration?"

"Horrid. He quit after our daughters were threatened. The newspaper sent him on leave for a couple of weeks, hoping things would die down. He was totally miserable not being able to write, so he started a blog under a phony name. He wrote about the same kind of stuff, though, and it wasn't long before the editor at the *Times* started publishing his material under a pseudonym. But the bastards figured out it was him and they arrested the editor and Jake quit. By then, I'd been threatened in person and had moved with our daughters and I filed for divorce."

"Wow, I'm sorry for everything you and your family have been through, Kate."

"We certainly aren't the only ones. I've heard such…tragic stories from other community members.

How did you and Juan end up working for Leo?"

"Juan worked for him when he was in grad school, then went to work for a private computer company until I got fired from the bureau. Then Leo hired him back. And Leo is brilliant, especially with AI. "I...I had hoped that when my daughters and I moved, all this bullshit would fall away from our lives. Talk about...about living in a fucking bubble." She shook her head.

"Honestly, I'm ashamed of myself now."

Luna heard the regret in Kate's voice and reached out and touched her shoulder. "Don't be so hard on yourself." She pulled into a parking spot at the market. "Let's go inside and do what we came here to do."

Even from the outside, the market looked like a sprawling one-story building with two separate wings. When they went inside, the vastness of the place was staggering. Everywhere she looked there were piles and stacks of food. Kate grabbed a cart. "I'm going to start shopping."

"Good. I'll find the owner or manager."

Luna walked off toward the front desk, where a pair of female clerks were busy waiting on customers. A third clerk came over to her. "Hi, what can I do for you, ma'am?"

"Is the manager around? Or the owner?" "The owner is out of town, but I'm the manager. Nora Newman."

"Great to meet you, Ms. Newman. I'm Luna Ochoa. Is there someplace where we could talk privately?"

"Sure. My office." She stabbed her thumb over her shoulder. "Come on back here."

Luna went behind the desk and she and Nora entered the office. Nora shut the door and gestured at one of the chairs. "Okay, this probably will sound strange, but I need to shop for a lot of people. Three hundred to be precise."

"You guys in hiding from the government or something?"

Luna suspected she assumed they were undocumented. Before she could reply, Nora continued. "Because we'd be more than willing to support you if you're trying to avoid deportation. It's just evil what these fuckers are doing."

An ally, Luna thought. "Many of these people were fired from their government jobs and others are people just fed up with the way this fascist government is murdering our rights. If you or your employees would like to join us, we have additional housing."

"That's kind of you, thanks. I'll talk to the others."

"We'd have to screen you first. Run you through our security AI system, Neptune, to check you're not secretly working for the other side. I hope you understand."

"Of course." Nora actually sounded reassured to hear it.

"Cool. So, the main reason I'm here is to make sure the community has a steady supply of food and we can pay for it, of course."

"Fantastic. Just give me the details."

"Another community member, Kate, is out there shopping now."

"We have a delivery truck. If you can just let me know what you will need each week, we can deliver it."

"Just in case the admin discovers where we are, I don't want you endangered. We can send a couple of vans to load up food."

"So these fuckers are really after all of you?"

Luna nodded, reluctant to say too much. So she also quickly explained about what was different about the community and how they worked. Then the front door opened and when she glanced around, there stood Izzy, all six feet of her, a stunning black woman with a body so formidable that when they'd worked together in the field, no man would take her on. She was also a crack shot.

They rushed toward each other, hugged, did a high-five. "I was afraid I'd missed you, Luna."

"No way. I told you I'd be here."

Kate approached them, pushing a cart piled so high with groceries that Nora hurried over pushing an empty cart and started unloading some of the stuff into her cart. "Nora, Kate, this is Izzy, a former colleague from the FBI. Nora is the manager here and Kate is a community member."

"Pleasure to meet you both," Izzy said.

"C'mon, Kate, I'll get you checked out," said Nora.

"Thanks," Kate said, and the two women pushed the carts over to an empty register.

"Izzy, I probably should mention that we're running an experiment with a very different system of government. One that really is democratic. You'll see when you join the community."

"You know, I heard rumors about this."

"You did?"

"Yep. The activists in my group have been discussing these ideas for a while and heard there was a platform being set up to facilitate democratic participation on a mass scale."

"That's right. Like Ancient Athens. In fact, we call it Athenia"

"Thing is, it's not totally new to this country either."

"Really?"

"Not at all. There have been 'Town Meetings' in New England for over a century. It's where the whole community comes together to discuss key issues and actually make policy collaboratively."

"Wow." Luna understood why she and Izzy were always such firm friends. Every time they met, Luna learned something from her.

"The only question is scaling it."

"And overcoming the inevitable resistance of the oligarchs." Luna reminded her.

"True. But given the destruction they are heaping on us these days, it's not a confrontation we can avoid anyway."

"You got that right. It's now or never. So how far is your, uh, group?"

"Group," she repeated, and looked slightly uneasy. "The thing is, since we texted earlier this morning, our numbers have swelled by another thousand. There's quite a solid underground of communication."

"Let me help Kate with the groceries and then you should follow us back to the community." Luna nodded toward Nora. "She may join us, too."

"And Izzy, I hope you understand, but first we'll have to run everyone throughout security AI, Neptune, to make sure there are no risks or moles," Luna explained.

"I understand. But we're still growing."

"That's fine. The process takes seconds per person. And we have plenty of space."

"Love it!" Izzy's expression was a mixture of excitement and relief.

* * * * *

Less than an hour later, Luna and Kate were headed back to the community with her more than $2700 in groceries. Behind her was Izzy's van with her first contingent. Many more would follow. What they didn't realize then was just how many they would be eventually.

* * * * *

Jake felt uneasy about this car trip back to Max's place. He lived in the middle of Orlando, in the Hourglass District of older homes, newer townhouses and a growing commercial area on Curry Ford Boulevard. In the past few years, vacant properties had been consumed by new construction. Now it boasted a large population of millennials who undoubtedly were paying huge interest rates, the result of this administration's policies, and wondering what the hell had happened to the rest of the American dream.

He had no idea whether this area was under the administration's scrutiny. But until he learned otherwise, it was safest to assume that the neighborhoods in here were being watched. Good ole Big Brother had been resuscitated - out of fiction and into the real world, just like *Handmaid's Tale.* Even the book burning from Orwell's classic *1984* had found oxygen in this admin. It wasn't widespread yet, but in time it would be if things continued along the present course.

And changing that course was what the community was all about.

"On the right, just ahead," Max said, gesturing. "Park in the garage. Safer."

Jake turned into the driveway as the garage door rose, and drove in. He stopped next to a VW van straight out of the 60s, an image of what you might find on the front of a hippie tee-shirt. "Let's make this quick," Max said, and got out, Jake right behind him.

As soon as the door swung open, all of Jake's internal alarms shrieked. The kitchen had been wrecked - dishes and glasses and coffee mugs shattered on the floor, the stove turned on its face, the fridge door open, food scattered everywhere, the glass shelves in pieces. The pantry door stood open and everything that had been inside had been hurled out with such force that canned goods had popped out, spilling tuna fish and clams, vegetables and fruits all over the place. Boxes of spaghetti had spilled open, glass jars of jam, spaghetti sauce, and Christ knew what else had been shattered.

"Fuckers," Max spat, and ran into the living room.

In here, the destruction was even worse. "Just

leave it, Max, and get the things you need."

"I'd like to know how these bastards got in."

"I'll look around. Just get your stuff so we can get outta here."

Max hurried for the bedroom and Jake quickly snapped photos of the destroyed kitchen, then moved quickly around the living room, checking the door, windows, even the floorboards. He ducked into a hallway and into one of the bedrooms and here, the lock on a back door had been shattered. He took photos of this too. Nothing else in the room had been touched, which led him to think the intruders had focused on the front of the house for the shock value. But to be sure, he opened the closet.

Nothing looked out of place in here.

"Hey, Jake, look at this shit!" Max shouted.

Jake hurried through the destroyed kitchen to the other side of the house, where Max stood in the doorway of a bedroom, a bulging backpack hanging from his shoulder, and gestured wildly at the far wall. Spray painted across it in bright red letters was: *U r so fucked*, Max, w*e r coming for u*

"They're the ones who are fucked, Max." Jake touched his arm. "They got in through the back door in another bedroom. You have everything you need?"

"Yeah, but I feel like I should clean this place up first."

"Leave it. That way if they come back, they'll believe you haven't been here."

"Yeah. Shit. At least they didn't find my cash." Jake took pictures of the wall. "You mind if I use these photos in my articles?"

"Use them. People need to see what these fucks do."

Before they went into the garage, Jake looked through the living room windows, making sure no cars were at the curb or in the driveway. Max joined him at the window.

"Looks clear out there."

"You have a security cam in here anywhere?" Jake asked.

He pointed at an eave. "Smashed."

"Did it grab any footage?"

"Haven't checked yet. I'll do it once we're on the road. I think it's clear outside, Jake."

They ducked out into the garage and got into his car before Max raised the door. Then Jake backed out quickly and forced himself to maintain the speed limit as he headed back through Max's neighborhood. He felt grateful that he'd cleaned out his place already, that his ex and daughters were safe in the community, at least for now.

Once they were on the way to the community and he could keep to the speed limit, he glanced at Max. "Checking the security cam?"

"Uh, yeah. It caught some stuff."

He texted the images to Jake and he brought them up on the navigator screen. Two masked men emerged from the hallway where Jake had been and began to systematically destroy everything in the room. They went after it with baseball bats, their boots, a broom, a mop, brass knuckles. Then one of the men glanced up and stabbed his arm at the ceiling. He lowered his mask long enough to shout, "Security cam!"

"Got it," the other man yelled, and fired his gun at it.

In the moment the first guy's mask was pulled down, Jake recognized him. The MIB. The little shit who had intended to frighten his ex some years back when Jake had surprised him and subsequently decked him. He must have been wearing lifts in his shoes, though, like the Florida governor often did, because he looked taller than Jake remembered. Jake paused the image, snapped a photo of the little shit, and emailed it the team - himself, Luna, Max, Leo, Juan. One way or another, they would find this little MIB shit.

"You recognize him?" Max asked.

"Yeah." Jake explained what had happened several years back. "I think of him as one of the admin's hired lackeys who shows up everywhere. He reminds me of some ephemeral fictional character who takes telepathic orders."

"Shit, maybe he does. Honestly, at this point, given what's happened to this country, I can believe almost anything is possible." He threw up his arms. "The ETs have landed! The goddamn aliens are running the government but they look human!"

Jake pulled to the side of the road and turned to Max. "All this shit is the result of selfish, greedy billionaires who hunger for power, Max. And somehow, a bunch of voters bought the president's lies and he became the head guy throughout the world and here we are. The people. These fucks are murdering our rights. I'm willing to fight for this. Are you?"

Max rubbed his hands across his face. "Yes, shit, I'll do anything."

"Good. Then I'd like to help you with these outlook teams."

"Don't you have to write the social media pieces?"

"The bulk is written. I just have to revise according to what we learn and as new info is turned up in events. Like the photos of what they did to your place. The sooner you get your outlook teams where you want them to be, the sooner I can release my pieces and the sooner we can put Athenia out there for the larger world."

"Wow. That's awesome to hear, Jake." Visibly excited now, Max's eyes lit up, his body became animated. He turned in his seat. "It's like this. The day that prick director of the bureau fired me, his glee was visible. He *loved* doing it, *loved* having the power to fuck up someone else's life. And my first thought, Jake, was that I was going to get even with him. But I realized that was my ego speaking and what I really craved was changing the system. Then he hired me back again because no one else could do the IT stuff that I do, and that's when I knew the path I would take." Max opened his arms wide. "So here I am, twice fired from the agency where I worked for more than twenty years and we're going to take back our rights, take back our country."

"Look, man, I'm just glad you're here."

"So I can help you out tonight?" "That would be great."

Jake pulled back onto the road. For minutes, neither of them spoke. Then Max got personal, which surprised Jake. "Any chance of you and Kate reconciling?"

"I doubt it. I'm just happy she and the girls are safe in the community. But even if none of this had happened, we probably would have ended up divorced."

"Why? "I guess because we're just too different."

"She and I talked for several hours in the past few days. It's probably nothing and I'm probably making a fool of myself just for thinking this but, well, I like her Jake."

"Then let her know."

"Really? It's okay with you? "Go for it, Max."

He suddenly laughed. "Christ, I can't believe we're talking about this while the government is crumbling around us. While we're on the road to fascism."

"We're going to block that road. We're a movement, Max. And movements change everything." He knew what else he wanted to say, hesitated, and then Max said it for him.

"Luna is like you, Jake, fired up and passionate and ready to leap in wherever she's needed."

Jake nodded, remembering that brief near-kiss, the brush of her mouth, how he'd felt at that moment.

"When you two are in the same space with me, I feel your chemistry. It's the weirdest thing. Maybe all this has kicked me into psychic awareness or something."

"Well, hey. If at the end of this you're with Kate and I 'm with Luna, you and I can still remain friends."

Max laughed and lifted his bare feet onto the dashboard. "You got it, dude."

TEN

Philips met his team of five in his tiny office in downtown Orlando, a private spot he'd rented some months ago when things with Olivia started going south. It was on a second floor, a cubby hole large enough for a desk, filing cabinet, bookcase, a couch and not much else. A small fridge under the window held some basic foods, water, a couple of sandwiches, several apples. The Five entered briefly, he handed out water, then they went to the garage downstairs and got into his SUV. His phone rang. It was Kumar.

"Hey dude. You on your way?"

Philips figured Kumar was fuming at the fact that the president had sent a message to him directly because it made Kumar feel undermined that the president hadn't gone through him. But that was exactly the president's modus operandi. He liked pitting his people against one another like rabid dogs.

"Yeah, I am and I don't have time to chat."

"Wait, wait. The president called me about it himself." Kumar, Philips thought, was peacocking.

Evidently he felt certain that he was the bigger alpha here since he'd gotten a call from the president himself and Philips had gotten a call only from the chief of staff.

But it made sense, Philips thought. Kumar was the instigator of the Nationwide Drone Surveillance Program in the first place. It was the best way they could locate, gain dirt on, and arrest every one of the people on his enemies list. A list he wrote up at the end of a book. A book the president just loved. "The president was irate."

"He was?"

"Yes. He's obsessed with finding out where those extra drones came from. He told me that 'only I am allowed to have so many eyes', which is right."

"Okay."

"So I'm calling you to pass that on. It's time to get them. So get out there, man, pull out all the stops, and find them."

He obviously said it in a way that encouraged him to answer with respect, something like *Yes sir* or *Yes, Mr. Director.* Instead, he hung up. "Good riddance, fucker," he muttered.

But as soon as he hung up, Sarah Wells called. While the other men got out of the car, Philips stayed and took the call.

"What's going on?" he asked.

"I think we're about to get an insider tip on the location of the traitors."

An inside tip? "Inside from *where?*"

"Supposedly from where they are."

"How do you know?"

"One of our agents has a handle on it."

"We're about to set out on our search of Sanford, air and ground, so keep me posted, Sarah."

"You bet. Look, be careful. The protests are spreading to almost every town and city now. There're not many places where it's safe for the administration to travel."

"Fucking country's becoming ungovernable."

"Well, that's down to us." Her voice raised. She sounded sour - didn't like hearing it. "You do your bit and I'll do mine."

Philips knew what that meant. He could even foresee the call she was about to make to Kumar. *Time to start getting violent with protesters, Pat. Military deployment might follow.* It was the moment, Philips knew, that Kumar had been waiting for his whole life. He could just imagine the expression of ecstasy on his squashed up face.

"Doing my bit right now." As he got out, the chopper that would be their eyes in the sky landed and the pilot, Chet, got out and hurried over. "Hey, Kevin, serious shit going down, huh?"

"Uh, yeah. You got the scoop?"
"From Sarah. Where do you want to start, Kevin?"

"Neighborhoods, the more innocuous, the better."

Chet touched his arm. "Get this. Remember that black woman, Izzy? She got canned in the prez's first wave of firings in the government."

"And? "She has a group of thousands who have joined the traitors." "Is someone in her group the snitch? Sarah mentioned an insider tip."

"Could be. Would make sense. Guess we'll know pretty soon."

"Well, until we do, here are the neighborhoods where I think we should start," Philips said, and got out his phone with the map on the screen and started pointing out the locations.

"We'll be in constant communication, Kevin."

179

Chet grabbed his hand, shook it, then abruptly turned and loped back to the chopper, where his two security guys were loading stuff into the chopper's belly, its cargo area.

He hurried back toward his car, suspicious now that Sarah's bit about an insider tip was her or the president's first step in setting him up to take the fall for – well, that drone that was shot down from 10,000 feet, or something else. *Take your pick.* Had Olivia been right about what she'd shouted at him when he'd left the house?

How many people had fallen already as a result of the president's order or actions? Right off, he could think of eight - four attorneys, two judges, the man who chaired his inaugural committee, one of his top fund raisers. There were more, but those eight were the most recent.

One of his attorneys had been sentenced to three years and was now in solitary confinement in Raiford, probably the worst prison in Florida. One of the judges…

"Stop it," he hissed, and knuckled his eyes.

* * * * *

Luna, Juan, Jake, Kate and her two daughters whipped up a late lunch/early dinner for dozens of people in the community and they ate outside, at four picnic tables under the old graceful banyan trees. Nika made the rounds, charming everyone, her tail whipping back and forth. For the first time since she'd left the bureau, Luna felt as if she belonged somewhere.

Everyone had brought something to contribute to the dinner. The community gathering was happening among the other houses as well, a chance for everyone to discuss their collective situation. She hoped others were feeling this same sense of belonging that she did.

Jake suddenly squeezed onto the end of Luna's bench. "How're you doing?" He spoke quietly, leaning in closer to her.

"Okay, all things considered. You?" "Same. I learned something interesting today. Max is interested in Kate. They'd be terrific together."

She realized that the revelation relieved his guilt about the mutual attraction between the two of them. She tapped his thigh with the back of her hand. "What else?"

"The MIB shit ransacked Max's place. He was on the security video."

"More scare tactics. You going with the lookouts tonight?"

"I don't know. First, the celebration in the plaza."

"Text me when you know."

"Definitely. Izzy and some on her team are going to join Max. I know that much."

A few minutes later, Max hurried over with Izzy. "There will be 20 of us," he said.

"Ten men, 10 women," Izzy added. "We'll leave after the celebration in the plaza. We're all a bit nervous about that drone that was brought down, but everyone needs a sense of togetherness."

"Once we're on the move, we'll report in periodically to Leo," said Max.

"And to you, Luna," added Izzy.

"My phone will be on and charged," she assured them.

* * * * *

Jake was impressed by the thousands that gathered in the plaza – the original members of the community plus Izzy's growing army. Leo stood at the microphone, testing it to make sure the pair of speakers worked.

"For those of you who recently joined us, I'm Leo

Montoya. When the president was running for election, I started buying up homes in this neighborhood in the event the man won. It's well contained, with a wooded area to the east and south and citrus groves to the north and west. Granted, it's not impenetrable. I-4 is only several miles from here.

"You see, every crisis is also an opportunity. I created this space, not just to protect us, but to protect future generations. It's not going to be good enough to just elect better people next time. We need a better system, and this is where it starts. You have all seen what a participatory platform like Athenia can do. Everyone plays a part in making decisions about their lives. Sure, we're small, but the same principles can be used, with the right technology, for communities and populations of any size. And today we are going to enable that. Today is the day we release Athenia to the world."

Surprised expressions all around. Everyone knew this was one of the priorities that they identified together, but now it was here, Jake knew it felt hard, collectively, to believe.

"Are we really doing this?" Juan asked.

"Well, the *Times* and other pieces are all out there now," Leo said. "Protests are building every day. They've spread to every city and almost every neighborhood. Half of the population are out on the streets, the country's slowly being brought to a standstill. The time is right, no?"

Jake sensed a realization spreading across the plaza. One or two nods became a dozen, then more and suddenly a thunderous applause erupted.

"It's time," said Luna.

Jake stepped forward. "Here's the message we've drafted to send out on social media, alongside the full code for Athenia. Bear with me while I read it:

"People are scared and want answers. But the answers to everything we need as a country, as a people, indeed as a species, are within us all. Each and every one of us. It's time to take back control. We don't trust the government to govern us anymore. At least, not on their own. Not without our regular and constant input and consent. More than just once every four years. We need to take the decisions themselves into our own hands.

"This platform is one way we can achieve that. The code will help you to set it up. It'll help you forge a new kind of network. One in which everyone has a say, and everyone shares and learns as they go. The technology will then help you to harvest the best ideas and find out where the consensus lies. It can feed into any electoral system you have. This really is for the people, by the people. Given what's going on in the

world around us right now, it really is now or never. It's up to you."

"Let's do this!" shouted an elderly Latino woman in the middle of the crowd. Several people started whooping.

"It's now or never!" shouted a teenage girl.

Then her friends joined in and after that it spread through the crowd like a virus. Jake, Luna, Leo, Max and Juan held hands in a chain at the front and raised them together as the whole crowd chanted, "It's now or never!" over and over.

Jake saw Leo's nod to the Hacker Collective at the back. This group of genuinely genius tech minds had spent every waking hour for months developing the platform. Now it was time to let it go and give it to the world. Off they went, without fanfare, to their stations.

A Rubicon had been crossed.

Max came over to Jake and gave him a thumbs up. Jake nodded back. It was time to start the lookout shift. As they brought the heat of the world upon them, this was now going to be a vital task.

"You ready to move out?"

"We'll go in by cars to our various lookout

points. No need to train Izzy or her group. A couple of them will be going with the newbies to take up lookout to the south, same for the west. The rest of us will be divided between the north and east, where we're most vulnerable. You got your gear?"

"In my car. Everyone armed?"

"Yup. And they all have gear," Max said.

* * * * *

Before the twenty of them divided into four cars, Max made introductions so they all knew each by first name and cell number. The ten women from Izzy's army of thousands looked as formidable as she did. They had enough room in the community for several hundred of them, and the rest lived nearby in airbnbs, condos, apartments, and houses, and some were camped nearby. Like everyone else, their phones were on.

Max's car led the procession, Jake followed him, and Izzy brought up the rear. In his car he had Juan, Ace, and two women from Izzy's group – Rebecca and Lynn, both of them former college professors fired from Florida universities when the president had decided to attack universities on their diversity policies. Rebecca was black, Lynn was a Latina. They had been among the first to join Izzy's group.

186

Max led them to a deeply wooded area near a small lake and then up a hill that, although shallow, provided a surprisingly clear view of the road that led in here and the surrounding land. They parked deep in the trees at the top of the hill and got out.

Max spoke to them by phone rather than using a mike. "I think there are certain rules to follow here. Mainly, that we're a defense squad, not a murder squad. I know you all have done this type of lookout work before in your various jobs, so you're aware of the protocol. Even though we aren't expecting any thugs from the administration to show up here tonight, we want to be prepared if and when they do show up."

Suddenly, on the open line, someone hissed, "This is Sam. There are four SUVs headed up the road toward us. Your call, Max."

"Take cover in the trees," Max said quickly. "Get as close to them as you can without endangering yourself. If they turn toward our neighborhood, we shoot out their tires. These banyans can be climbed and having additional altitude can give you some leeway. Stay on this channel, but go on mute. Texts from here on out."

With this, everyone started moving and Max and Izzy fell into step with Jake. "You sure you didn't arrange this as a training exercise, Max?" Izzy whispered. "I remember when we worked together briefly at the bureau you used to arrange stuff."

It was news to Jake that Max and Izzy had worked together at the bureau. "You two will have to explain this to me later. After we've won."

Izzy snickered. "He trained me in special forces."

They caught up with Sam and stretched out on the ground with him. He had binoculars glued to his eyes and the rest of them pulled out their binocs. "See them?" Sam whispered. "Their license plates tell us they're government vehicles."

Yeah, Jake saw them, four SUVs with darkly tinted windows, moving steadily but slowly, maybe 35 m.p.h., because the road wasn't paved or well lit. They were approaching the fork in the road where the route to the right circled eventually back toward Orlando. And the route to the left led to the community about ten miles in.

"I think it's time to make sure they don't take that road to the left," Max said softly.

"Shoot out their tires?" Izzy whispered.

"Uh-huh. Let's do it," Jake said.

"To the count of three," Max said. "One...two...three..."

The explosion of gunfire echoed through the moonlight, a deafening sound but deeply satisfying, Jake knew, for all of them. And one by one, the SUVs swerved, ran off the road, stopped. "Lay low," Max warned, and a moment later, those SUV doors flew open and armed men leaped out, firing wildly, scuttling around like swarms of ants or termites.

* * * * *

Philips, in the lead SUV, knew the gunfire had flattened his front and rear tires on the right and turned abruptly away to the left. Into the trees. He grabbed his phone and his pack. He threw open the door and scrambled out and took off into the woods, running so fast he could barely catch his breath. Behind him, the gunfire continued, but it was closer now, his men firing back. *Fools, you goddamn fools. Take cover.*

How many of them would end up dead? How would Sarah Wells spin this so it would look like *he was at fault, that he'd acted without authority,* that he'd taken matters into his own hands... Well, he had. Five men, divided between two cars.

He didn't have any idea what had happened to the three men in the SUV that had been following or to the two who had been in the car with him. He didn't much care, either. Right now, it was all about self-preservation.

189

But he didn't have any idea about where he was.

He slipped out his phone and keyed in the GPS map. His location pulsed red. He appeared to be in the middle of a vast wooded area north of Orlando. It was hard to read the damn thing while he ran, so he stopped next to a tree, pressed back against the thick trunk, and caught his breath. He tried to read the map.

Nearest town: Cassadaga.

Great. A Spiritualist community. The place where everyone spoke to the dead. He remembered a song called *Four Winds* with lyrics that included: *...went to Cassadaga to commune with the dead. They said, 'You'd better look alive.'*

He didn't need a psychic medium. But he needed to look alive. He also needed a fucking car. His phone buzzed, the pilot's number appeared on his screen. "Chet, you see something?"

"My instruments registered gunfire. What's going on?" Philips quickly explained. "Can you tell where it came from?"

"Fuck yeah. Hilltop just above where you all were."

"Stay in the area. There has to be a neighborhood somewhere nearby." "Yeah, there is. Shit, shit, you aren't going to believe this. Sarah just texted me the coordinates the snitch gave. She told the prez and he ordered the launch of two dozen armed drones. The coordinates are uncomfortably close to where you and I are. Start running, Kevin. Head for Cassadaga. I'll pick you up there."

He ran faster than he'd ever run in his life and hoped to hell he would find a car with keys in the cup holder.

* * * * *

Everyone in the community heard the gunfire and Luna's phone blew up with text messages. A text came in from Jake: *high alert 4 suvs, we shot out their tires, the people inside scattered.*

The next text came from Izzy. *Backups from my gang are on it, spreading out along the road but they're reporting drones headed our way. We're taking cover.*

Everyone in the house took up positions at the windows, upstairs and down, with both Luna and Kate at the front windows in the living room. No one had discussed the possibility of something like this, but they were as prepared as they could be, armed and ready.

Minutes later, an alarm sounded on her phone

and Kate's, three rapid screeches. *Drones in the vicinity. Take cover.*

"Take cover where?" Kate exclaimed. "I can see one of them. It's too close. We'd never make the cellar in time." "Kitchen pantry. No windows. Where're your daughters?"

"Cellar."

"Text them to stay put."

Kate, texting madly, took off for the pantry and Luna glanced outside and up again, spotting the drone as it neared them. She texted Leo. *Can Neptune disable it?*

Yes. But more than 24 appear on radar. Neptune can get closest one & maybe the one right behind it, but then may have to reboot.

More than two dozen drones? WTF?

Suddenly, the front of the closest drone dipped forward, then it spun toward the ground and vanished. A breath later, Luna heard the crash.

She texted Jake. *1 drone down. Where are you?*

Pursuing Philips w/Max. Izzy & Juan on their way back w/3 of Philips crew. Other 2 are dead. More drones spotted. Take cover in cellars.

Shit, shit. She shouted for Kate, called her dog, and the three of them headed for the cellar. But then a call from Izzy came through and Luna made sure everyone on the cell line could heard it. "Luna, almost there, got three fuckers."

Luna tore back upstairs. "I'll unlock the doors. Hurry up."

Minutes later, three men staggered into view and in the moonlight they looked ragged, worn, defeated. Behind them were Izzy and Juan. Luna unlocked the door, threw it open.

"We need a place to put these guys," Izzy said, breathless, excited. "They were in Kevin Philips's group."

"Cellar," Luna said and pointed her weapon at the three. "Forward, assholes. Fast."

"Can it be locked?" Izzy asked.

"Yes."

"What about the windows?"

"Secured," Juan said. "Leo and I did that yesterday."

"Great," Izzy said, and down the stairs they went.

"What the hell are we going to do with them?" Juan whispered.

"Find out what they know."

Kate, her daughters, Nika, and a dozen other people who lived in the house were already there. The cellar was large, with three windows that looked out toward the front of the house. Luna was pleased to discover that the hurricane impact windows were securely locked. They looked fairly new and she wondered if they were also installed on the rest of the windows in the place.

Some stuff was stored down here – extra bedding, several bare mattresses, cushions from an old couch, towels, but nothing that could be used as a weapon. They tossed the cushions on the floor and the three men sank onto them. Juan hurried back upstairs to get cold bottled water for them. Plastic bottles that wouldn't even dent these windows if they were thrown.

Nika started barking at the men. Izzy pointed at a security cam in a corner of the ceiling. "Leo must have the app for it."

"Well, we need it, too," she said, and texted him. She gave him an update, took photos of the three men, sent it along with the text.

Need to download the app for security cam here in cellar so we can monitor it. Where r u? Monitoring radar two houses down from you. I'm seeing another 22 drones headed this way. Link attached to what radar is showing and to security cam in your cellar.

Moments later, the links appeared on her phone and she texted it to Kate, Juan. The entire community. *Stay safe, Leo. Intend to. Make sure u & all the others do too. Keep me posted on news from Jake & Max.*

She ended it with a thumbs up.

ELEVEN

Jake and Max found the lead car, driver's door wide open. The two men inside were dead - one from a gunshot, the other from a head wound - and Philips was nowhere in sight. They trotted along the left fork in the road, which eventually led to their neighborhood.

It turned out that Max was a terrific tracker. He shone his flashlight on the heavy boot prints in the dirt and they followed them for a couple of miles until they abruptly ended. Max turned in place, like a dog sniffing the air for a specific scent and headed for the trees. Here, he picked up tracks that looked as if Philips had been running.

"Looks like something spooked him," Max remarked, the beam of his flashlight pinning those footprints.

Jake consulted his GPS, looking for the nearest actual town. "Cassadaga lies about two miles straight through those trees."

"Then that's the closest place he's likely to find a vehicle to steal," Max said. "I say let's follow those prints and see what we discover."

"I'm game," Jake said.

So they kept moving through the trees, Max in the lead until he suddenly stopped, staring at his phone. "Uh, text from Leo. Izzy brought in three guys from Philips's team who are still alive. They're in the cellar of the main house. Do we want to go back?"

"We want Philips," Jake said.

The prints were steady and consistent and brought them to a wide street with a brightly lit hotel on one side, several houses on the other. They stood at the edge of the trees checking the street, then moved toward the hotel. As they got closer, Jake heard music - piano music that sounded live - and laughter from a large group of people on the hotel's front porch.

Let's join them," Max suggested. "Maybe Philips is mingling with them until he can convince a taxi to pick him up here."

"I thought taxis picked up anywhere."

"The Florida governor has issues with Spiritualism - it's not Christianity, after all - so some of the cab companies stopped covering the area. They don't want to piss off the governor and get slapped with a fine or something."

197

"That's an actual threat?"

"Yeah, that asshole actually sent out a directive to the Orlando bureau to that effect."

"He and the prez sound like soul brothers," Jake remarked as they headed toward the hotel.

"Yeah."

"So FBI agents are supposed to arrest any taxi or Uber drivers who work this town?"

"Uh-huh."

"That sounds illegal, Max."

"The governor, like the prez, doesn't give a shit about laws."

The lights on the hotel porch were bright enough for Jake to see that the group numbered a dozen or more. Then, suddenly, he saw Philips at the edge of the crowd, yucking it up with a woman, a blonde. "There, see him, Max?"

"Yes. What do you want to do?"

"Let's join him on the porch. See what he does."

They made their way through the crowded parking area, trotted up the several steps like they belonged, like they were guests at the hotel, and quickly blended into the noisy crowd. The lobby door was open and music from the jukebox inside drifted out, loud and fast and pounding now, definitely a recording. Two couples were dancing, the women obviously professionals, and some in the crowd clapped to the Latino rhythm and cheered them on.

A waitress came over to them with a tray of drinks and Jake and Max helped themselves to ginger ales. "Everyone at the dinner party is entitled to a free reading with Helen, inside at the bar," she said.

Jake nodded. "Thanks."

"Make us look like we're part of the dinner party, Jake. Go inside for a reading. I'll keep an eye on him out here."

Jake snapped a photo of Philips cozying up to the blonde at the far end of the porch. If nothing else, he could show it to the psychic and ask her take on it. He enlarged and cropped it. "Text me if something changes."

"Yeah, yeah, of course."

Jake slipped inside the hotel lobby. He remembered reading that the hotel had been built in the 1920s, in the heyday of seances, mediumship, and psychic trickery. The rich and the famous flocked here in the winter months and the Spiritualist camp grew up around that influx of visitors. The lobby did look old, with garish wooden flourishes on the ceiling, lace curtains on some of the windows, and signs everywhere about how to get a psychic reading.

The last window to his right had a Venetian blind that was pulled up halfway, enough for him to catch sight of Philips still on the porch, his back to the window as he embraced the blonde. So, who was she? A girlfriend? A convenient pickup? If so, maybe he hoped she would invite him to stay for the night, a good hideaway for a few days.

To his left was the dining room and a sign in the doorway read: *Dinner Party Psychic Inside.* He texted Max. *Going into dining room 4 reading.*

Ask about dipshit.

Plan to.

He's moving in on blonde, maybe 4 a place to stay 4 the nite?

My thoughts exactly.

BTW, Izzy reports that she's going to interrogate the 3 men who are locked securely in cellar.

Jake carried that thought into the dining room with him and sat down at the bar. It was quieter in here, the loud speaker apparently was turned off or the jukebox had been unplugged. A brunette at the other end of the bar was talking to a young man who kept nodding his head, then set a pair of $20 bills on the counter. "Thanks so much, Helen."

Helen the brunette tucked the bills in the pocket of her jeans and came over to him. "Hey, how're you doing? I'm Helen."

"Jake."

"So would you like something to drink, Jake, or a reading or both?"

"Just a reading, thanks."

"You're with the party outside?"

He nodded.

"Do you have a specific question?"

Is the takeover of the government going to be successful? Are we going to get out of all this alive? Will my relationship with Luna develop? Will my daughters be okay? Will my ex end up with Max? So many questions. But the one that mattered the most right now... He set his phone on the counter and turned it so that Tammy could see the photo of Kevin Philips that he'd snapped just before he'd entered the building.

"What do you pick up about this guy?" He turned on his cell's recorder.

Helen, whom Jake guessed was in her mid-forties, leaned forward, elbows propped on the counter, her necklaces dangling, and studied the photo without touching the phone. After a few long moments, her vivid blue eyes raised to his. "I'm going to be blunt."

"Good," he said.

"He's a fucker. And he's a danger to you and the people around you." She pressed the fingers of her right hand against her temples as if to stem a pounding a headache. "Right here. He shoots someone right here." She squeezed her eyes shut. "Jesus...this guy, I've seen him before...somewhere..." Her eyes snapped open. "He's in the president's administration."

Angst and horror rolled away from her in waves, and Jake quickly slipped the phone back toward himself and turned it over so the photo of Philips was no longer visible. "I'm sorry, I didn't mean to upset you."

The hand at her temple dropped and gently covered his, which rested on the counter next to his phone. "There's a woman..." She smiled at that. "You wouldn't believe how many times a day I say that to men. There's usually a woman. And for women, there's usually a man. But in these times, new alliances emerge in the strangest ways. This woman's name is unusual. She understands who you are and what you're doing….And that man in the photo on your phone…is a danger to her. To you. To your family…daughters, you've got two daughters and that monster is a threat to them as well." She paused, bit at her lower lip. "This fucker is a threat to all of us."

Suddenly, explosions tore through the air-distant, closer, then practically on top of them. Panicked screams and shrieks on the porch prompted both of them to hit the floor, then Jake scrambled on his hands and knees around the end of the bar until he was behind it with Helen. He zipped his phone in shirt pocket. "What the fuck," she whispered.

"Stay low." He reached under his shirt for his weapon and moved toward the door to the dining room/bar. An employee, a guest, someone - had shut it, perhaps locked it as well, and the handful of people in here now cowered under tables, behind chairs, behind and under anything that might protect them.

Jake grabbed the door handle, shoved it down. Nothing. Outside, the panicked shrieks continued. More explosions. Helen shouted, "That's close! Like, right in Spirit Lake!"

Now he heard distant sirens. He bolted upright,

turned the dead bolt at the top of the door, and it swung partially open. The screaming drowned out any sound he made. He slipped out the door and into the lobby, saw employees hiding, heard frantic pounding on a door at the other end of the hall that opened onto the long porch that ran along the right side of the hotel. Terrified people seeking a hiding place, a refuge, safety.

Jake quickly went to the main door and, through the lace curtain that covered the window, saw the chaos outside, people stumbling out into the street, arms thrown over their heads, tucked at their sides, grabbing others to protect them as they scrambled away from the porch. He threw open the dead bolt on the door and rushed outside.

He stumbled over two bodies on the porch, jumped over another on the stairs, and ran out into the road after Max, who chased Philips up the street. People on either side of them raced off in the opposite direction. The sirens now closed in and Jake ran harder, faster, and as he got closer to Max, shouted at him to duck. He did and Jake took careful aim at Philips and fired.

He missed.

A car turned suddenly onto the road, screeched to a stop next to Philips and he jerked open a door and threw himself inside. The vehicle took a sharp 180 in the middle of the road and tore away from town. Jake scrambled to his feet, helped Max up. "That was Moe's car," Max exclaimed. "The MIB. Shit."

The cellar air felt tight, almost breathless to Luna. She, Juan, and Izzy stood in front of the three men, firing questions.

What had Kevin Philips told them about their mission?

What were they doing in the woods?

What had Philips hoped to find?

What were Philips's intentions?

It went on like that for 10 or 15 minutes, each of them firing questions at the men. And invariably, the responses were predictable: *I don't know. We weren't told. Philips never says much. We were following orders.*

"Orders to do what?" Luna snapped.

Silence.

"Hold on," Izzy said, patting the air with her hands. "You were following orders but don't know what those orders were? How the fuck is that even possible?"

More silence.

Weighted, thick.

"You were threatened?" Luna asked. "By Philips? The president? Maybe the VP? So you're all cowards?"

One of the men snapped, "Maybe you all aren't aware of it, but the president has been firing people from the government every day and we're just trying to keep our goddamn jobs, okay?"

"By doing illegal things?" Luna snapped.

"According to the president and Philips, you people are domestic terrorists,"

"*We're* the terrorists?" Juan exclaimed and exploded with laughter. "Dudes, you drank the proverbial lemonade."

"The presidents and his administration are attempting to turn this country into an autocracy," Izzy said. " A dictatorship."

Luna spoke up, struggling to keep her voice calm, measured. "He has trampled the bill of rights. He's trying to silence the press, has protesters arrested, is deporting immigrants to notorious prisons in other countries and does it without due process, ignores court orders, has gutted social security, Medicare, Medicaid, and is cancelling federal money for universities that don't fall in line with what he wants.

He's pulling money from FEMA, obliterated the Department of Education, gutted the FAA which already had a shortage of air traffic controllers, gutted NOAA...you know, the weather agency that keeps us informed about hurricanes six months out of the year... Should I go on?"

Now the men looked extremely uncomfortable, glancing at each other. One of the younger men suddenly started weeping. "My son...is autistic. Without Medicaid, his...his condition is getting worse. When I said that to...Philips, he promised to...to take care of it."

One of the other men snorted with disgust. "And you know that's a fucking lie, David. Philips lies about everything."

"His intentions are good," said the third guy.

The first man shouted, "Aaron, his intentions suck! My grandmother is 93 years old and can't survive without social security. She had to move in with my parents. If I told Philips that, would he promise to fix social security? Of course he would. But he doesn't have any say over social security or Medicaid or any of the other agencies that he claims he had done something about. It's all bullshit!"

"Okay, okay," Luna said, patting the air with her hands. "Hold on. We've all got gripes here. Could you guys tell us your names?"

The man who had just blasted Philips for his false intentions spoke first. "I'm Andy. I've worked in the domestic terrorism unit since the president was elected. I've yet to meet a domestic terrorist - except the president and his staff, they' re all terrorists!" Then his voice broke with emotion. "I've hated this...this job since day one. But I needed the work. My wife's pregnancy is...complicated and our insurance company cancelled us and I... get insurance through this job."

"What about you?" Izzy asked the man next to Andy.

The man looked at Izzy with such despair in his eyes that Luna nearly rushed forward to hug him, to pat him on the back, to assure him everything was going to be okay. Except she couldn't assure him of that. "I'm Carlos. I'm Cuban. I...I came here as an infant in the Mariel boatlift. I...I...got fired from the school where I taught...Spanish because I wasn't born here. Philips hired me because he...needed to use someone who spoke Spanish. I was...desperate for work. But when I saw what they were doing I tried to back out. Then they threatened to send me to a South American torture chamber. Everything I've seen...is like my...my mother's stories...of life under Fidel..."

Juan went over to him, squeezed his shoulder.

"Amigo, tienes una casa aqui, con nosotros. Juntos, vamos a establacer una democracia verdadera. Pero esta vez va ser una democracia verdadera, donde todos pueden participar juntos en decisionaes. Una empieaza nueva."

Luna translated what he said for anyone there who didn't speak Spanish. "Friend, you have a home here with us. Together, we're going to start again, create a new society with a new way of running our government and democracy. A new start."

Carlos looked at him, tears gathering in his dark eyes. "*Gracias.* Anything will be better than this. I want to join your movement. May I join you?"

"Me too," echoed Andy.

Aaron, who had said that Philips's intentions were good looked uncertain, scared. "You want to continue working for him?" Kate asked. "For this administration?"

"I...I..." His voice cracked, he looked on the verge of hysteria. "I...hate the man. I hate the entire fucking administration. But...but I need this job, I....support my mom, my wife, my son..."

"Excuse me," Leo said, and trotted down the cellar stairs. "I've been listening to all this at the top of the stairs. We'd like you gentlemen to join us. Can someone please unlock their cuffs?"

Izzy went over to them and freed their hands. Juan got bottles of water from the small fridge and Kate helped hand them out. Then Leo said, "Here's the situation. Those drones are armed and attacked Cassadaga. Jake and Max got out and are headed back here in a car they stole."

"Where're those drones now?" Luna asked.

"Headed here," Leo said quietly.

Second later, a series of explosions all around them triggered such panic in the cellar everyone dived for the floor. Several windows shattered. The house itself shook. Luna, sprawled on one of the cushions, covered her head with her arms. More explosions shook the air and now screams could be heard from outside.

Leo nudged her and she raised her head. He held his computer on his lap and she could see drones and other craft on radar.

"What...are they?" she whispered, her voice cracking.

"Armed planes," Neptune said.

"Everyone get under the stairs!" Leo shouted. "Or the couch, into the storage room, fast!"

They all rushed for cover but there wasn't room under the stairs for everyone, so Luna, Juan, Leo and several others threw themselves in the storage room, Luna slammed the door, and moments later more explosions. Then everything went black.

PART THREE

Ashes

"Only in the darkness can you see the stars."

Martin Luther King Jr.

TWELVE

Chet picked up Philips and Moe in the chopper just outside of Cassadaga, then flew them to Orlando where they transferred to a private jet for D.C. that was owned by a business associate of Chet's. Philips was so exhausted, he couldn't utter a word. Apparently Moe felt the same. The only voice was Chet's. "We should be in D.C. in less than two hours. So relax while you can."

Relax. Christ. Philips had stumbled over bodies on the porch and knew the attack from the drones or planes or whatever they were had killed even more people. Why had they struck so far north of Sanford? Or had they also attacked Sanford?

He pushed up from his chair and moved to the front of the Gulfstream. The pilot's door was open and he went inside, settled in the co-pilot's seat and slipped on the headphones. Chet looked over at him.

"You look like shit, Kevin."

"Feel like shit. What do you hear out of DC?"

"Silence. I've texted Sarah multiple times, but no

answer."

Not good, Philips thought. It meant she might not know what the hell was going on, either. Or that she'd been instructed to keep it to herself. "You mind if I text her?"

"Mind?" Chet laughed. "Fuck, no. Let's get an answer so I know whether to land there or not. Otherwise we may be flying into total chaos."

"Was Sanford attacked?"

"Yes. The only reason I know that is because of other pilots. Parts of Sanford are obliterated." Philips texted Sarah. *Barely got out of Cassadaga. WTF is going on?* She didn't answer immediately. "Chet, can we circle around until she responds to my text?"

"You bet. I'd prefer that."

The jet turned steeply to the right and Philips peered down at the land below. Northern Florida, southern Georgia, he guessed. From here, the world looked calm, serene, and some visitor from outer space might be led to believe that the U.S. would be a fine place to settle in. He suddenly wondered where his wife, Olivia, was.

He texted her. *Hey, where r u? Things ok?*

It elicited an almost immediate response from her.

OK? Are u fucking kidding? As soon as I heard there were drones sighted, I left the house and headed out of goddamn Florida. Where the hell r u? Still doing the president's bidding, Kevin?

Trying to find out what's going on.

Ah, right. Well, I can tell what's going on. @ the moment I'm sitting in a gas station off I-75, hoping there's enough gas left to fill my fucking tank. Headed to my agent's place in Atlanta. 1000s of cars on the road, everyone fleeing. Remember the evacuation before Ian slammed into us?

Ian, Hurricane Ian. His tired brain struggled to go back into the past. Ian, 2022. Okay, now he had it. Initially, Ian was supposed to hit the east coast of Florida, where he, Olivia and their son were visiting at the time. A short family holiday that had gotten cut much shorter as the Cat 5 hurricane had approached South Florida.

They'd packed up the car and headed out, back to Orlando. But as it turned out, six million other people had also decided to evacuate south Florida. The largest evacuation ever of the state. The gas stations on the turnpike had run dry. Cars along the turnpike were pulled onto the grass or sometimes just dead right in the middle of the road, tanks dry. A trip that should have taken them three hours had taken nearly eight and by then, Ian had taken a turn to the west and was hitting Florida's west coast and its winds and torrential rains were forecast to head inland, over Orlando.

Beyond that, he didn't remember much except statistics, facts. Ian was the costliest hurricane in Florida history, even surpassing Irma in 2017. It devasted Sanibel Island off the Florida west coast and dumped so much rain and caused such extreme devastation that some people were trapped on west coast islands for days. He was pretty sure now that in the aftermath, his and Olivia's marriage had collapsed and it was why their son wanted nothing to do with them.

Hey, Kevin, u still there?

Yeah I was stuck back in Ian.

OK, getting gas. Will be in touch @ some point. Don't take the fall 4 fuckhead.

Wait.

He could almost hear her thinking, *Wait for what?*

Olivia?

Yeah?

I'm sorry, 4 everything.

Little late for that, Kev, but...@ least now I have my next book

"Kevin?" He looked from her last words to Chet.

"Yeah?"

"Asshole has declared martial law. I'm not landing in DC. Going back to Orlando."

"Martial law for *what?*"

"He's saying country is being hijacked by terrorists."

"Terrorists?"

"I think he means the protestors."

"You mean the peaceful protestors who haven't damaged anything or hurt anyone this entire time," Philips murmured.

The plane banked sharply to the left, turning back for Orlando, and Philips immediately wondered where the hell he should hide. Not the house, not his office. Downtown Orlando would be empty, people evacuated to wherever. And forget hiding out in Cassadaga. There probably wasn't much left of the town, not if Spirit Lake had taken a hit. It was just down the road from the hotel.

His phone dinged. A text from Sarah. Finally.

217

Kevin, we're now under martial law. Too much chaos in the country. Not just here in DC but all over. People have started rioting in streets since the announcement, millions headed out west – somewhere, who the fuck knows where?

Where r u?

Outta here. Not going down with this fucker. Europe looking good. Get out while u still can, Kevin.

He read this last text to Chet, who glanced over at him. "I'll let you off in Orlando, Kevin, if that's where you want to go. But I won't be sticking around."

"Where're you going to go, if not there?"

"Canada. Toronto. Where my sister is."

"Would she take me in too?"

"I'll ask. But what about your wife and son?"

Well, yes, there was *that.* But his son didn't want anything to do with him and at this point, Olivia probably considered him too toxic to help. He couldn't blame her. "They hate me, Chet."

His expression wasn't exactly sympathetic but Chet seemed to understand his dilemma. "Okay, Toronto it is, man. But I can't make any promises."

"Yeah, I get it."

Some message came through and Chet touched his right earphone. He hit a switch on the main instrumental panel so that Philips could hear what he heard, the voice of an American Airlines pilot.

"This is AA Flight 915. It looks like we are all in a formal mayday situation now. An official press release from the White House states that the president is considering a nuclear strike on the country he believes is responsible for the drone incursions on American in recent days. He insists it must be an invasion and that America must retaliate. He doesn't name the country. Nonetheless, NATO has gone on high alert. South America has gone on high alert. Africa just went on high alert. Asia, too. The map on my screen shows that even Antarctica has gone on high alert. I'm headed for New Zealand, and just hope I have enough gas to get there. Over and out."

This communication has gone out worldwide. "Fuck," Chet spat. "This goddamn prez and his administration are going to start world war three."

"I can't believe it."

Philips knew this was the end of the line for the multitude of true believers like himself, except that he had never been as true and dedicated as Kumar or others in the administration.

"Well, you'd better believe it," Chet retorted. "And you better believe that meanwhile he and his billionaire buddies are all hunkered down in their bunkers somewhere, partying for tomorrow."

Philips rubbed his hands over his face. Then, from behind them, Moe's voice: "Did you hear?"

"Uh, yeah. World War Three," Philips muttered.

"Uh-huh. So where're we headed?" Moe asked.

"Not New Zealand," Chet said. "Not enough gas, this plane doesn't have the capability."

"How about the space station?" Moe suggested.

Chet laughed and Philips was shocked he still had the capacity for laughter. "Wrong craft, dude. I'm headed to Canada."

"Then so are we," Philips said.

"But if asshole actually launches a nuclear attack, we'd have to be close to the Arctic to be safe," Moe remarked.

Chet nodded. "Yeah. We would. And we won't be. But it's better than sticking around here."

Philips repeated a phrase from *Star Trek.* "Make

it so."

A long time after the explosions ended, everyone in the cellar came out of hiding and gathered in the center of the room. Luna thought it looked bad, but it could've been much worse. Scattered all over the floor was shattered glass, chunks of concrete that had fallen from the ceiling, and parts of bushes blown through the windows. A tree had fallen against one of the windows and leaves and broken branches lay clustered at one side of the cellar.

"You think it's safe to go outside?" Luna asked.

"Wait, hold on," Leo said, fiddling with his phone. "Holy shit. The headlines. My God. The president has announced his intention to nuke the country he believes is responsible for the drone incursions. He's apparently sure it was a foreign agent but hasn't named the country. All the NATO countries have gone on high alert."

"It could just be another one of his lies," Juan said.

"Maybe," Leo conceded. "But if it's not, this is going to trigger a nuclear war. It may be time now to head to those tunnels."

"Not without my people, Max, and Jake," said

221

Izzy.

"Any word from them?" Luna asked.

Izzy shook her head. "Not yet."

"What tunnels are you talking about?" asked one of the three men from Philips's group.

Andy, Luna thought. That was his name. "Under Disney World. An entire world of tunnels."

"But getting to Disney from here…" Carlos bit at his lower lip. "The interstates and roads are going to be jammed with cars. The nukes could start flying before we even get there."

"I'll text my brother," Leo said. "See what he suggests."

While he did that, Luna and Kate headed for the stairs. They needed to get outside, see what kind of damage there was. But when they reached the door at the top of the stairs, it wouldn't open. Luna threw her weight against it and the door opened slightly, enough for her to see debris piled against it. "Hey, is anyone out there?" she shouted.

"Luna?" called a man on the other side of the door. "That you?"

"Yes! A bunch of us are down here! Who's

this?"

"Ace. Hold on, I think we can move some of this stuff so we can open the door enough for you all to get out."

By now, everyone was crowded at the foot of the stairs, and Leo and Juan stood on either side of Luna and the three of them slammed their bodies against the door simultaneously. The people on the other side pulled at the same time and the door gave.

Luna, Juan and Leo stumbled out into what looked like the aftermath of a hurricane. Kate followed and the four of them stood there, horrified by what they saw.

The front of the house had been blown out, part of the second floor had collapsed, and Luna could see that the street was filled with debris. "Injuries?" Leo asked.

"No fatalities," Ace reported. "A couple of minor injuries. The docs are tending to them. But the community..." He shook his head. "We can't stay here."

"Any word from Jake? Max? Izzy's group?" asked Luna.

"Yeah. They got out and are nearly here. They said they've been trying to call and text you all, but the connections are all bad."

They made their way through the debris to the street. People were wandering around, sifting through debris, obviously in a state of shock. "I heard from my brother," Leo said. "We're welcome to stay in the tunnels. But getting everyone there is going to be challenging. How many vehicles do we have? Anyone have an exact number?"

"We have thousands," Izzy said. "And every group that joined has at least one vehicle, some have two. We have enough vehicles. "

Luna texted Jake. *How far out are you?*

A mile.

We're going to the tunnels.

Wait 4 us.

She ended with a heart.

Minutes later, two cars appeared at the end of the main road, unable to get through the piles of debris. Luna loped to the cars and hugged everyone as they got out. She hugged Jake tightly and he leaned back slightly and ran his fingers through her hair and brought his mouth to hers.

"You heard?" she asked.

"Yeah. Nut case is going to nuke the country responsible for the drones. It was all an excuse for him to start a fucking nuclear war."

"They call it accelerationism. End the world so they can start again," Jake recalled.

"Freaks."

"We need to look after ourselves and the community now. The tunnels are a great option, but we'd better hurry up. Get people alerted and out of here. "

Leo, Izzy and others now joined them. She saw Kate hugging Max, then Jake's daughters hurried over and threw their arms around him.

"I sent a group text," Leo said. "Everyone is going to meet in the plaza in half an hour and decisions will be made on who's riding with whom. My brother suggested that we arrive in groups of five cars and park in the underground garage. He'll be outside to direct us in."

"Any update on the president's nuclear threats?" Max asked.

"Not yet," Luna replied. "But we should all stay attuned to local and national news."

"Are these tunnels big enough for over 3,000

people?" Izzy asked.

Leo's head bobbed up and down. "Since some of the Disney employees are joining us, we figure our numbers are going to be much higher, maybe five thousand of us. Gary assured me the tunnels can accommodate up to 8,000 people."

"But are these tunnels far enough underground to protect us from nukes?" Izzy asked.

"Unknown," Leo replied and opened his arms wide. "But it's obvious we can't stay here."

* * * * *

"Hope you guys have passports with you." Chet glanced back at Moe, then looked at Philips.

"Yup," Moe said, "Always got mine with me."

"Same," Philips said.

"My sister tells me that since the president was elected, Canadian immigration has gotten very fussy about who they allow into the country. So like I said earlier, there aren't any guarantees."

"Not even for you with a sister who lives there?" Philips asked.

"Oh, there won't be a problem for me. I have a Canadian passport."

Philips and Moe exchanged a glanced. "I didn't realize that," Philips said.

"Got my citizenship a decade ago, when my sister married a Canadian. She suggested it, just in case we got a prez like this one."

"What happens if they don't let us in?" Moe asked.

"You'll have to rent a car and drive back to...well, somewhere."

"There may not be a somewhere to return to," Moe said, voice laced with panic.

"Any more news from anywhere?" Philips asked.

"Not yet." Chet fiddled with the radio. "Wait. Here's something. Reception sucks, but..." He turned up the speaker so both of them could hear whatever it was.

"This is Air New Zealand, Flight 568. We have just been denied entrance to Australia because it's on lockdown in anticipation of a nuclear strike."

"Roger, Air New Zealand. This is Delta Flight 1230 en route to Spain. We've been told we won't be permitted to land in any NATO country due to a possible nuclear strike from the U.S. We're declaring an emergency and asking permission to refuel in

Portugal."

"We hear you, Delta. This is Quantas Airlines, currently headed to Quito, Ecuador. We've been denied entrance..."

"Is Canada going to allow us to land?" Philips asked.

"I got clearance earlier. But all this is recent. I'm going to check."

He contacted the Toronto tower "Toronto tower, this Cessna Citation, flight 111. Are we still permitted to land in Toronto?"

"Flight 111. You were granted permission earlier and that permission stands as long as the airport remains open. What's your ETA?"

"About 90 minutes."

"Good. We'll be closing in two hours."

"Why are you closing?"

"The president of the U.S. is threatening nuclear war. The prime minister has ordered the airport shut by eight p.m. tonight."

"What types of preparations are being made?"

"Underground shelters are open all over the

country. People being told to stock up on food and supplies. Over and out."

"Jesus God," Moe exclaimed.

Philip's cell rang. Sarah Wells. He walked out into the passenger area to take the call. "Sarah. Where're you?"

"On my way to Costa Rica. Europe is out. What about you?"

"Headed to Canada."

"They may let you in if you tell them you worked for the nutcase prez. That's what I did to get into Costa Rica."

"Any word yet on a nuclear strike?"

"I really think he's going to do it."

"What the fucking fuck?"

"Well, he'll be safe. And guaranteed a place in history. It's all he cares about. His family and all his buddies are in bunkers too."

"Why aren't you in one?"

"You kidding me?" Sarah sounded disgusted. "Spend my last months and years cooped up with that lot. I'd honestly rather take my chances."

Long pause.

"Good luck Sarah."

"You too."

After they disconnected, he stood there for long moments, his head pounding, his thoughts rushing around. So many *what ifs* they kept slamming into each other.

THIRTEEN

Now the news came in fast and furiously – on Jake's phone, on the radio, on the phones of the others in the car who were on different websites and apps. And none of it was good.

Martial law declared in the US, military deployed

Tens of thousands of protesters arrested or shot across the southeast by US military

National Guard deployed in 30 US states

US citizens go into hiding

Canada's border closing at 8 pm. Mexico border presently shut down.

Flights to and from US closed worldwide

Worldwide shipping halted

Sales of US bonds tank

Stock market crashes

World democratic leaders recoil in horror

Retaliatory strikes being planned by every nuclear

nation

Numerous billionaires en route to planned hideouts: private islands and bunkers around the world.

One horrifying headline after another was followed by frantic emails and texts from friends and colleagues. This was the archetypal coup that had happened in Hungary, Chile, Venezuela, Russia, North Korea, the list was so long Jake nearly got lost in it. Only this time a nuclear war was thrown in. But when he glanced in the rearview mirror, he saw his daughters, Kate, Max, Luna and Juan in the back seat.

Leo led the procession, Jake was second, and behind him was a train of other vehicles, 50 or 100 of them, and behind the first group were another hundred or more. In all, he figured there were at least 500 vehicles that would fill the garage where Leo had suggested they park. He suspected the Disney lot would be empty by now, that tourists and visitors had heard the news and were rushing to make preparations to keep themselves and their loved ones safe. So if there was an overflow, they could park in the lot.

As they approached the Disney garage, he spotted Leo's brother, Gary, waving both arms, then directing them inside. He held a megaphone. "We'll be escorting you into the tunnels in groups of 50 to

232

100". Initially, it was going to be smaller groups, but the reports out of D.C. were becoming more dire and urgent by the minute so they sped things up.

He parked next to Leo 's SUV and they all got out with a bag over their shoulders and a backpack. Fifty in the community followed Mickey Mouse down two flights of stairs, into and out of two elevators, and finally emerged in the area they had entered the day Gary had shown him around.

He took Luna's hand. "How far underground do you think we are, Jake?"

"Maybe 75 or 80 feet."

"Is it deep enough?"

"To avoid death? Radiation poisoning?" He shrugged. "No fucking idea, Luna. But it's preferable to the Sanford neighborhood. And better than Cassadaga."

Mickey Mouse took them into one of the long halls. "Please, choose your room, leave your belongings there. There are larger rooms that sleep four or more for families, but also triples and doubles. No singles, sorry. Our crew will be bringing in the vast amounts of food you all brought with you. Now, if you'll excuse me…. I need to help Leo escort more people into our facility. Any questions?"

"Yes," called Nicki, one of Jake's daughter. "Is there a map of this place?"

"Wow, my bad. There's an app." He gave the URL from the Disney employee site. "With that map, you'll be able to find whatever you need."

With that, Mickey hurried back the way they'd come. "You want to bunk with Kate and your daughters?" Luna asked.

"I think my daughters would like a room of their own." He tilted his head toward his ex-wife and Max. "I suspect they'll end up with a double too." He looked at her. "And us?

Luna laughed, a soft, seductive giggle that Jake felt he'd been waiting to hear his entire life. "Let's go find our room."

* * * * *

The Cessna Citation touched down at 8:01 p.m. at the Toronto Airport. Philips felt nauseated about what might lay ahead, but struggled to maintain an even, mildly optimistic mood. After all, right now, he was out of the USA and the president and his sycophants couldn't touch him. Or Moe.

Chet taxied to a spot at the corner of a terminal and emerged from the cabin in his pilot's jacket, a bag hanging at his side. "So let's take our next step, gentlemen."

Next step. Yeah, okay. Right foot, left foot, over and over, up the aisle, down the steps and toward the building. Toward immigration. Moe fell into step beside him as they approached immigration. "Hey, Kev, what's your assessment? Will you and I get to stay?"

"Sure. Because we tell them who we worked for and how much information we have to share with them."

Moe snapped his fingers. "Just like that, huh?" "Maybe not that easy, Moe. But it's not despair, either."

"At least not yet."

They followed Chet to the counter, where he spoke in French to the immigration officer. That pissed Philips off. But on a lighter note, a more optimistic note, maybe it was just a matter of courtesy,

"Passports, please."

Chet handed over his Canadian passport, Philips and Moe handed over their American passports. The immigration guy stamped Chet' passport, handed it back to him and motioned him to the other side of a low metal fence. Then he looked at the American passports, glanced at both of them, and texted on his phone. Three men who were obviously police – but not dressed like any cop Philips had ever seen - hurried over to them.

"Please come with us, gentlemen." A handsome man in his early forties spoke first,

"Is there a problem?" Philips snapped.

"There are questions," Handsome Dude replied.

"What kinds of questions?" Moe asked.

Handsome Dude rolled his eyes and the man next to him, brown hair and eyes, said, "Come with us, please." They were escorted to a room adjacent to the immigrants and told to sit down at the table. "We know who you gentlemen are," Handsome Dude said. "You both worked for the dangerous American president."

"What are his intentions? Is he going to start a nuclear war?" a second official asked.

Then the third man spoke up. Philips guessed he was the one in charge. "Is he hoping to ruin the world above ground so that his billionaire friends in their bunkers can someday claim it as their own? Is that how this story is supposed to end?"

Story? What story?   What was this guy talking

about? "What're you referring to?"

"Yeah," Moe said. "You guys think this nuke threat is just a *story*? Is that it?"

Guy in Charge leaned in across the table. "Mr. Moe. Our lives are stories. Your life. Mr. Kevin's life. My life. The lives of all my fellow officers. The lives of every Canadian citizen. You know where I learned that truth? From a book by a Canadian author that your country banned. *The Handmaid's Tale.* By Margaret Atwood."

Uh-oh. Olivia had read the book, seen the movie, watched the TV show. Atwood was poison. Philips knew they were fucked.

"We...we..." Moe stammered.

"Shut up, Moe," Philips snapped.

Moe went silent. "We'd like to see your prime minister," Philips demanded. "We have information to provide."

"Well, Kevin, our prime minister has no interest in speaking to either of you. We will drive you both to the border and let you out."

"Let us out *where?*" Moe shouted. "Upstate New York in the middle of nowhere?"

Guy in Charge didn't respond. He nodded at the other two men, who grabbed them by the arms and escorted them out of the room and out of the airport to a waiting police car.

Fifteen very long minutes later, the cop car pulled to the border control, spoke something in French, and they were waved through. Just on the other side, the driver got out – armed but not threatening – and gestured for them to get out.

"Welcome to Niagara Falls, gentlemen. It's a long trek to Buffalo but I'm sure you can find a ride."

He and Moe stood there like a couple of lost souls as the driver made a U-Turn and headed back over the border.

* * * * *

As exhausted as Luna was, at every level of her being, she felt she'd arrived at her final destination. Pieces of herself were strewn across central Florida – in the bureau, working with her brother for Leo, meeting Jake, the birth of the community, the AI, and now this. Now here she was, unsure about whether she or any of them would survive. And when you believed that, believed it deep within yourself, it changed all the silly rules.

So when Jake collapsed on the bed beside her and

they found each other's hands, she knew that if she died in the next hour or the next minute, it wouldn't matter. For right now, for this second, this breath, this heartbeat, she'd found home.

Then the bed started to subtly vibrate. Jake sat up.

"Your phone," she said.

He reached into his pocket and held the phone out so she could read it too. A message from the Hacker Collective: *User numbers for Athenia rising exponentially, in every continent. Military big wigs in chains of command in a number of countries using it too. Collaborating to try and abort launches wherever possible. Communities forming across the globe. Engagement soaring.*

NOW, IT'S OVER TO YOU

Our aim is to bring Athenia to life. An app that will enable all of us to easily and quickly play a part in the decisions of government. An app that will pool our collective intelligence, so that we can make better choices, by doing so collectively.

But we need your help to make this happen. A share of the profits from this book will be used to develop Athenia, so by recommending it to others you will help us to make the change.

Beyond that, if you have any ideas or skills that can help us develop Athenia – whether in admin, ideas about the design, the technical aspects of development or helping with engagement and promotion - then we want to hear from you. Visit the website below and join us.

Finally, its adoption will depend on political leaders who champion and add this, or at least the general concept of participatory democracy, to their platform. That's why we need to spread the word among Congress men and women, Senators, Governors and even future presidential candidates.

We therefore ask you to forward the book and these ideas to anyone with power and influence you might know and let us know of any positive feedback you receive in this regard. I (Russell) would be happy to join any conversation that's started this way.

Also, if you're in other countries, we'd love to see approaches to leaders, representatives, MPs and Ministers around the world too.

Ultimately, we can no longer leave it to a small group of politicians to do and decide everything for us. Whoever they are, even despite their best abilities and intentions, we know now where it will lead. It's therefore down to all of us to literally be the change we seek, turn the page and create a better tomorrow together.

Now, it's over to you...

www.ReadWeThePeople.com

Printed in Dunstable, United Kingdom